CONSTANCE VERITY
DESTROYS THE UNIVERSE

ALSO BY A. LEE MARTINEZ

Constance VERITY

DESTROYS THE UNIVERSE

A. LEE MARTINEZ

— BOOK THREE —

SAGA PRESS

LONDON · SYDNEY · NEW YORK · TORONTO · NEW DELHI

SAGA PRESS

AN IMPRINT OF SIMON & SCHUSTER, INC.

1230 AVENUE OF THE AMERICAS, NEW YORK, NEW YORK 10020

To Mom and Sally,
To the DFW Writers Workshop,
To Walt Simonson,
And to you, because they wouldn't pay me if
you didn't read 'em.

CONSTANCE VERITY
DESTROYS THE UNIVERSE

1

C onnie's trip from Shangri-la had taken longer than expected. The ox ride had gone smoothly, but her plane had been delayed and she'd missed a connecting flight. She'd made up some time by calling in a favor and hitching a ride on a fishing boat, but she was still running behind.

She'd told Byron not to bother waiting for her, just in case she didn't make it. She didn't expect anyone but Chestnut the Wonder Dog to be waiting for her in the condo when she arrived, but she wasn't terribly surprised when she found a pair of alien envoys also there. It was shaping up to be one of those kinds of days.

"You could have warned me," she said to Chestnut.

The envoy that was a mass of writhing tentacles with four eyestalks cooed over Chestnut. "Your companion beast has proven most engaging."

"I bet."

Connie turned over a couch cushion to find a gold-plated

ionic crystal, which she handed to the envoy. "Does this belong to anyone?"

"Oh my," said the envoy. "How did that get there?"

"It's a mystery."

Chestnut had sticky paws, acquired under an unscrupulous animal trainer. Connie had yet to break the wonder dog of her larcenous habits. Connie snapped her fingers, and Chestnut ran into the bedroom.

The second envoy, a vegetable-based hominid, rattled its leaves. Connie had a working knowledge of plant-ese.

"Blessed Snurkab, we come on matters of great importance."

Connie tossed her fur-lined hat on the coffee table. "Great, but can we skip the honorifics and get to it? I'm on a schedule."

"We apologize if this is an inconvenient time," he shook. "We wouldn't have come—"

"Yes, great importance, I'm sure," said Connie. "Do you mind if I change while we talk?"

The aliens followed her into the bedroom, but she shooed them out and shut the door. Chestnut sat on her dog bed in the corner, and Connie thought about turning over the bed to see if any other alien objects had wandered into the golden retriever's possession, but she was on a schedule. She stripped out of her dirty clothes. Byron had prepared an outfit for her on the bed. Just a shirt and some pants, but it saved her some mental energy, so she made a note to thank him later.

"Talk. I can still hear you."

"Well, honorable Snurkab," said the tentacles, "as it is known that you are the most trustworthy and honorable being in the universe, we have come to you because . . ."

She half listened as he explained the situation. A sacred artifact had been found, and several different civilizations were vying for control of it. An interplanetary war was brewing, and it had been decided by several wise leaders that the artifact should be kept in safe hands while negotiations were underway. There was more to it than that, but she stopped listening after a point.

She checked herself in the mirror. Her hair was a tangled mess. She ran a brush through it with mixed results. She sniffed herself, and she smelled like ox and sweat and raw fish. A shower would be prudent, but she didn't have the time. She applied deodorant liberally, gargled a capful of mouthwash, put on some perfunctory makeup. It'd have to do.

She opened the door. "Yeah, sure, I can hold on to your artifact for a bit."

The plant shook. "You are as gracious as—"

She pushed her way past them. The tentacle alien brushed her, leaving a bit of goo on her pants. She thought about grabbing a paper towel to wipe it up, but time wasn't on her side.

The envoys produced a barbed dagger made of shimmering metal. They bowed, presenting it to her. It was warm to the touch and vibrated ever so slightly.

"This isn't radioactive or cursed or anything?" she asked.

"Radioactive? No," said tentacles. "It might be cursed."

"Did we fail to mention that?" said the plant. It curved its leaves sheepishly around itself.

"Whatever," said Connie. "Is that all?"

"Yes, we cannot express in mere words our gratitude—"

"No need. Now, if you'll excuse me."

The envoys disappeared in a flash of teleportation. She tried putting the artifact in a purse, but she discovered she couldn't let go of it. It whispered promises of conquest and glory. She saw herself on a throne of skulls, ruling a thousand worlds.

"Maybe later."

She was in her car when she got a phone call. She shouldn't have answered it, but she assumed it would be Tia or Byron checking on her progress. She struggled to hold the wheel, dagger, and phone.

"I'm on my way," she said.

"Verity, we need your help," said Agent Ellington.

"I'm busy."

"It's an international crisis."

"It always is."

"Listen, Verity," said Ellington. "As your official liaison, I'm mostly stuck cleaning up the aftermath of your messes. And I do it without complaining."

"You complain about it a lot, actually."

"I still do it. You owe us."

"Why do I owe you?" asked Connie. "I'm the one who is out there saving the universe."

"And we make it easier for you to do. I know you've got things to do today, but this shouldn't take you long, and it's on the way."

"How do you know where I'm going?"

"It's my job to know," said Ellington.

"And if I say no?"

"We both know you won't."

Yes, they both knew that.

Twenty minutes later, Connie pulled up to a restaurant surrounded by special agents. Agent Ellington waved Connie past security.

"Whoo, Verity," said Ellington. "What is that smell?"

"Destiny," said Connie.

"What's with the bat'leth?"

"Just another favor I'm doing for someone else. It's a cursed alien weapon that thirsts for blood, so you might want to avoid getting on my bad side."

"Noted."

Inside the restaurant, a handful of customers and employees were lined against one wall while a corpse lay slumped over a table.

Ellington explained, "His name was Werner Neumann. Top scientist in the research of biological weaponry. Two hours ago, he stole a sample of an omega-level genetically modified virus from a laboratory. Thirty minutes ago, he was found like this."

"Shit, did you bring me into a contamination zone?"

"Relax, Verity. If the virus had been released, you'd already be dead."

"That's a comfort."

Connie checked Neumann. "He's been poisoned." She pulled back his eyelids and lips. "The distilled toxin of a rare South American blood orchid, otherwise known as the death bloom. A dose can be fatal in seconds to minutes, depending on method of delivery. My guess, don't try the soup."

She put a napkin over the bowl.

"Don't really care how he died," said Ellington. "Just need to know what happened to the stolen virus."

"Getting to that. The blood orchid is the poison of choice for a death cult that believes the world should have ended in 2012 and is out to correct that mistake."

"Like Aztec religious nuts?" asked Ellington.

"They're an international organization," said Connie. "You'll want to arrest the busboy and that woman in the hat."

The busboy shoved something into his mouth and fell to the floor, foaming and twitching.

Connie threw a wineglass across the room and knocked the suicide pill from the woman's hand.

The agents jumped on her.

"How'd you know, Verity?" asked Ellington.

"As much as I'd like to take five minutes to explain, I'm on a schedule. I'll give you the breakdown later."

"We still need the virus."

Connie bent over a potted rubber plant, dug out a small metal vial, and handed it to Ellington. "Don't lose this again."

Connie jumped into her car. She still had time. Traffic was light. She'd make it. She always made it. Almost always.

A black SUV tagged her bumper. Hard. Before she could dismiss it as an accident, it happened again.

Two more SUVs moved into position on either side of her. They rolled down their windows, and goons in ski masks leered at her.

She jammed the gas pedal.

"I can make it."

"Durodoye, party of nine," said Tia. "We have a reservation."

The host glanced up from his reservation list. "We only seat full parties, miss."

"One of our party is just running a little late," said Tia. "She'll be here."

The host made a noncommittal, but slightly displeased, noise. As if he worked in the highest-end restaurant, rather than a place that justified selling overpriced fish tacos by employing minimalist decor and putting vests and ties on the waitstaff.

The host adjusted his own tie. "We'll see what we can do."

Tia thought about slugging the guy. He was just doing his job. He didn't have to be a jerk about it, but then again, maybe he did. People probably paid more for the passive-aggressive tone.

"He's seeing what he can do," she said to Byron.

"We could push it back a little if you like," replied Byron.

"Oh, Mom would love that," said Tia.

Behind her, Zoey was sitting on one of the leather couches in the waiting area. Beside her was Harold, her second husband. And she was not happy. Between Mom and the host, Tia felt caught between the Scylla and Charybdis of disapproval. But she only had to worry about one of those dangers tomorrow. Whichever one was the whirlpool, she decided. Her mythology was rusty.

She turned to the host and placed her hands on his podium. He didn't like that, but she withstood the withering glare.

"I know your policy, and believe me, we will have a full party. And even if we don't, I will personally order two plates of whatever your most expensive item is if you seat us now."

The host smiled, savoring the power. He waved over a server, who guided them through the crowded, decadent world of trendy tacos to their table.

Hiro pulled out Tia's chair for her. He sat beside her and kissed her cheek.

"Shouldn't you be sitting with your folks?" she asked.

"We're not that close," he replied.

His mom and dad and sister sat at the far end of the table. It still struck her as odd that the world's greatest ninja/thief had such normal parents. His mom was an office manager, his dad a pediatrician. Neither of them spoke much English, but that saved her the trouble of trying to make conversation beyond exchanging bows and nods of acknowledgment. They seemed nice.

His sister, Sayuri, was long and lean with short black hair and enticing black eyes. She'd gone to the same ninja school as Hiro, though her specialty was vague. Something about fighting a secret war against time sorcerers or cyborg vampires. Hiro had advised Tia not to ask too many questions about it, and she'd taken the hint.

Byron left the seat beside Tia empty and sat next to Zoey and Harold. Harold, bless him, was trying to manage Zoey's dissatisfaction, but it was a losing battle. She drummed her fingers on the table. Another fight about Connie was brewing.

"I'm on it," said Hiro without Tia saying anything.

He went over to Zoey and Harold, inserting a chair between them. He said something charming, like he could, and flashed a smile. Zoey laughed and patted him playfully on the shoulder. Mom didn't approve of much, but she liked Hiro.

He winked at Tia from across the table, and she blew him a thankful kiss. She could handle this. They could handle this. It was just a casual dinner to celebrate their upcoming nuptials. No big deal. Not like the world depended on it.

"I'm sure Connie would be here if she could be," said Byron.

A server appeared and asked if they could have Connie's empty chair.

Connie flung open the doors. All heads turned toward her, perfunctory makeup running down her face, her hair and clothes drenched, as she walked through the crowd.

"Do you mind? I believe that's my chair."

The server retreated as Connie plopped into her seat. She

brushed her hair out of her eyes and used a napkin to dry her face and neck. She dropped the soaked napkin on her plate and kindly requested another.

"Sorry I'm late. Car chase. Had to park the car in a fountain a few blocks from here. You know how it is."

"Never doubted you for a second," said Tia. "You smell like destiny."

"Should've smelled me before the fountain."

"Just glad you made it," said Tia.

"I brought a change of clothes," said Byron. "Just in case you might need it."

Connie kissed him. "What did I do to deserve you?"

"Saving the world once or twice is probably enough," he replied before going to retrieve the suitcase from the car.

Zoey frowned at the scene caused by Connie's entrance, but Hiro whispered something in her ear. She laughed and squeezed his arm.

"Nice knife," said Tia.

"It's technically a dagger, and I was planning on getting the steak."

And even though the place didn't serve steak, Connie and Tia laughed anyway.

The rest of dinner went as expected. Connie couldn't change her shirt, since she couldn't let go of the alien conquest dagger, but at least her pants were dry. Hiro kept Zoey from making a scene. Connie kept the oversized dagger under the table to avoid confrontation, and the restaurant staff was happy to skirt an incident.

Afterward, everyone parted ways in the parking lot. Hiro left with his family, and Zoey and Harold went to retrieve the car, giving Connie and Tia a moment together.

"You look tired," said Tia.

"Thanks."

"I wouldn't have minded if you'd left early."

"Are you kidding? Wouldn't have missed this for the world."

"I should have gone with you," said Tia.

"No, you shouldn't have. I've gotten along on hundreds of adventures without a sidekick. It's nice to have someone around I can rely on, but you have a life. You're busy enough as it is. Consider this my wedding gift."

"My offer still stands. Hiro and I can push the wedding back if it's inconvenient."

"When is it ever going to be convenient?" said Connie. "I can keep the galaxy from catching fire for a few more days at least."

A shadow moved across the sky as a spaceship several blocks long hovered over the city.

"This is probably for me," said Connie.

A towering reptilian warrior materialized in front of her. Zoey and Harold pulled up in Tia's Honda Accord. Zoey glared from the passenger seat.

The ten-foot-tall alien, dressed in shining crimson armor,

removed her helmet with a loud hiss. Her tail swished, clanging as it knocked a dent in a streetlight.

"So this is the Snurkab of legend?" asked the alien. "I don't care what the rest of the universe says about you, I see an insignificant fool unworthy to carry the glurbakashah."

Zoey reached over and jammed the horn three times as she impatiently waved Tia over.

Tia opened her eyes wide and mouthed an exaggerated, *Give me a minute.*

Connie held up the alien dagger. "If you're here for this, I can't let it go. And I made a vow to watch it anyway, so I wouldn't give it up if I could."

Byron came over. "Is there a problem, honey?"

"No, I'm on it. What's the deal here? Are we going to fight for it?"

"Once the glurbakashah has chosen a champion, it can only be satisfied by the spilling of blood." The warrior drew a sword and leveled it at Connie. "I challenge you, Snurkab. You can't refuse."

"Okay, but not here," said Connie.

The warrior lowered her sword. "As you wish."

"Do you need my help?" asked Tia.

"No. I've got this."

Zoey honked again, and Harold slapped her hand. They started fighting. Even with the windows rolled up, Tia could hear them trading jabs. It'd be a long ride back to their hotel.

"Please, let me come fight aliens to the death with you," said Tia.

"Maybe next time."

Connie hugged Tia.

"Standard intergalactic ritual combat rules?"

"Of course," said the alien warrior.

"Great. Shouldn't take more than a half hour." She kissed Byron. "I'll meet you back home."

Connie and the alien dematerialized in a flash.

Tia drew in a deep, cleansing breath and marched toward her car.

Connie, covered head to toe in rancid alien ichor, materialized via matter transmitter in her living room.

"Hey, honey," said Byron, approaching with a cup of warm tea. "How'd the death match go?"

"A lot of buildup and then all the stabbing and stuff." She took the tea and sipped it. "You are a lifesaver."

"I do what I can."

Chestnut pawed at her nose and left the room.

"I need to wash the destiny off," she said.

"I wasn't going to say anything," said Byron with a smile. "I put out fresh towels."

She paused on her way to the shower to get rid of the glurbakashah. Now that it was sated on blood, she could finally drop it. It was an ancient relic of intergalactic conquest. It was probably dishwasher safe.

She jumped into the shower and let the warm water run down her face. All the alien sludge was bound to be hell on the pipes, but she'd worry about that tomorrow. Byron loosened his tie and threw his jacket in the hamper.

She traced a heart in the steamed-up glass and winked at him. "You look like you could use a shower yourself."

"Really? After the day you've had?" he asked. "I would think you'd be too tired for . . . showers."

"You would think," she said, "but nothing like a little blood duel to wake a girl up. Still coasting on adrenaline, but I don't know how much longer it'll last, so I wouldn't waste the opportunity if I were you."

He was in the middle of stripping out of his pants when a flash and low hum announced the materialization of the tentacle alien envoy in the bathroom. Byron was forced to sit on the toilet to avoid its slimy limbs.

"Blessed Snurkab, I hate to bother you, but I seem to have misplaced my precious scwoob and—"

The emissary averted its many eyes from the naked primates. It politely swallowed its retch. "Is this a bad time?"

"Is this it?" asked Byron, holding up a multidimensional object that was either a cube or a sphere, depending on how one held it in relation to the cosmic axis. "I found it under the dog bed."

"Many thanks. I promised to bring one home for my off-spring. My mate pairing would've been most dissatisfied if I'd returned without it."

The alien dematerialized with a soft pop, leaving behind a small puddle of slime.

"I'll get the mop," said Byron.

"It can wait."

Connie grabbed him by the collar and yanked him into the shower.

2

In the New Hebrides Trench lay a hidden entrance to a secret that had been waiting to be discovered since shortly after the dawn of the universe. The submarine emerged from the water into the vast underground cavern, carved into the earth by an ancient race long since vanished. Patty Perkins and Reynolds stepped onto the ground. They took in the massive temple, as large as a mountain, that filled most of the cave.

Reynolds fiddled with a sensor device. "These readings are promising."

Patty Perkins said, "We don't need promises. Is this it or not?"

He wasn't the kind of man to give answers he didn't have. He kept working at his device and muttering to himself.

The small stone shack just beside the temple opened its door, and the last Guardian emerged. The Guardian stood twelve feet tall and resembled a cross between a wolf, a cow, and several animals that couldn't be found on Earth, so there was no reason to mention them. She took in these strange, unexpected visitors from the submarine.

"Oh, I'll be right with you. One second."

The Guardian retreated to her shack. She found her ceremonial armor, covered in dust. There was no time to polish it, and she cursed her lack of preparation. But it had been forever since she'd had any visitors. Hundreds of thousands of years at least. Time was impossible to track down here, and she'd long ago stopped trying. She'd put on a few pounds over the eons, but she managed to squeeze into her armor.

She'd misplaced her sacred spear. She considered going on without it, but it really did complete the look. She'd been stationed here too long to blow it now that it was actually time to do her job. She was certain her people and their empire had long ago faded to dust, but on the small chance that they were still around, she didn't want a write-up. Her work ethic was all she had at this point.

She found the spear after rummaging blindly under her bed. The sharp point poked her in the palm, so she wrapped it in a hasty bandage and rushed out again.

The visitors stood where she'd left them. The man was still engrossed in data interpretation, while the woman was talking on her cell phone.

The Guardian rushed forward and prepared to give her speech. She'd rehearsed it thousands of times. Reciting it was as easy as breathing. Easier, since her breastplate was constricting her chest a touch.

"Hail, seekers!" shouted the Guardian as she thrust her spear forward.

Patty held up an index finger and turned her back on the Guardian. "Yes, I know it's lousy reception. I'm several miles underwater. It's the best we can expect. Oh, I don't know how. Reynolds created some special pills that are keeping us alive. Don't know how they work, but that's not my department. Yes, the satellite death ray launch is on schedule. Just waiting for the final payment to clear."

The Guardian deflated and leaned against her spear. She could wait, though it was a tad unprofessional.

Patty, a tiny little thing only about as tall as the Guardian's knee, ended her call and turned her attention to the temple. The Guardian moved to block Patty's view and launched into her speech.

"Hail, seekers!" shouted the Guardian as she thrust her spear forward. "If you are worthy, you will find death in this sacred place. If you are not, then forbidden knowledge and . . ."

She paused and ran it through her head again.

"If you are worthy, you will find forbidden knowledge . . ."

She set her spear across her shoulder and ran through it in her head.

"Is it 'find' or 'discover'? 'Discover' sounds better, right?"

Patty opened her mouth to speak, but the Guardian shushed her.

"No, no. I've got this."

She straightened and resumed her spear-thrusting stance.

"Hail, seekers. If you prove worthy, then forbidden knowl-edge shall be yours. If you prove unworthy, then only death awaits you.

"Know this," said the Guardian. "When the universe was still burning . . . smoldering . . . no, burning in the chaos of its birth, my people had already discovered its secrets. We saw the signs of the countless lesser species across the stars. But born too soon, we also knew the cycle of oblivion would claim us before they arose, as it claims all.

"And so, we took the Key and because we could not destroy it, because it could not be destroyed, we hid it in this place, where none would find it. And we built this temple of trials around it. And I was set here to stand watch and guide those who dared think themselves capable of claiming its terrible truth. Let me save you some trouble."

The Guardian glowered down at Patty and Reynolds.

"You are not worthy."

The Guardian stared into the distance to illustrate her contempt for the latest seekers.

"But you're welcome to try."

Patty adjusted her glasses, sized up the Guardian and the massive temple behind her.

"No, thanks."

She and Reynolds started back toward her submarine.

The Guardian trotted after her. "Wait? What?"

"Ancient temples of death aren't really my thing. But you are telling me the Key is in there, though."

"Yes, placed in the center with utmost care, surrounded by a thousand tests of strength, intelligence, and courage to ensure that only the most capable successor would lay claim to it."

"Terrific." Patty typed a text on her phone. "Sounds like a lot of trouble."

The Guardian lowered her giant spear. "So you're not even going to try?"

"You just said we were unworthy."

"It's only fair to warn you what you'd be up against."

"Very kind of you," said Patty. "Which is why I think I'll give it a pass, if it's just the same to you."

The Guardian said, "It's not that dangerous. Not really."

"Still not in my wheelhouse. Nor his. Right, Reynolds?"

He glanced up. "Definitely not."

The Guardian said, "It's not strictly ethical, but I could give you some hints. At least for the first few traps. The first one is pretty simple. It's all about prime numbers and—"

"No, thanks."

The Guardian jumped in front of Patty and Reynolds.

"Can I do something for you?" asked Patty.

The Guardian twirled her spear. "We went to all the trouble of building this thing, and I've spent countless eons watching over it, and the secret inside is really terrible and wonderful and amazing. And it feels like a waste if someone doesn't at least try it once."

"Nobody's tried it?"

The Guardian shrugged. "You're only the second to ever find it."

"So somebody has tried it, then."

The Guardian nodded toward an alien skeleton at the bottom of the stairs. "He tripped and broke his neck. Couldn't believe it. The stairs aren't even a trap. Mind you, they're a little steep."

Patty said, "Tell me, honestly. Do either of us look like the type of person who could successfully navigate a gauntlet of death?"

The Guardian measured the short woman and the thin man with the handlebar mustache. Neither was much to look at, even if the Guardian lowered her standards.

"No."

"Thank you for your honesty." Patty and Reynolds returned to her sub.

"Tell your friends about us!" shouted the Guardian. "We're always open!"

Patty waved over her shoulder without looking back.

The Guardian marched back to her post and sat at the foot of the stairs as the submarine sank into the water. The pool rippled sometime later—time was such an abstraction down here—as a small drone rolled onto shore. The Guardian approached the robot.

"Hail, seeker!"

The drone beeped steadily as a display counted down from ten.

"Well, that's just perfect," grumbled the Guardian.

From the submarine, Patty dispatched the excavators. It'd take a few days to dig out the cavern, but all things considered, it was the most efficient solution.

A severe bald man appeared on her screen. "Mrs. Perkins, I trust I can expect delivery soon."

"Very soon, Mr. Cassowary," she replied.

Smiling, she checked a status report projection and enjoyed her Long Island iced tea.

3

The next morning, Connie slept in. She rarely got the chance. She was pleasantly surprised to wake up with Byron beside her. She rolled over and put her arm around him. She snuggled up next to him and nibbled his ear.

"Morning, beautiful," he said softly. He couldn't fool her. He'd been awake for a while and had just been waiting for her to slide up beside him. He loved that. She loved that he loved that.

He turned around and wrapped his arms around her. They snuggled for a while more before Chestnut the Wonder Dog interrupted. She pushed open the bedroom door, carrying her leash in her mouth.

"I thought we agreed to lock that door," she said.

"I did," he said.

"We've got to get a better lock," said Connie.

"The installer said it was absolutely dogproof."

"You asked him if the lock was dogproof? And he just said yes?"

"He did give me a funny look before answering."

Connie smiled at him and chuckled.

"Yeah, like that," said Byron. "You're the one who brought home a larcenous dog."

The retriever, having already hooked the leash to her collar, set the handle down on the bedside table, along with the doggy bag dispenser. Criminal tendencies aside, she was very well trained.

"I don't suppose we could let her walk herself," said Byron.

Chestnut perked up.

"Oh no," said Connie. "Don't even think about it. If we let that dog loose on society unsupervised, we could be talking about a crime spree."

Chestnut lowered her head and flashed big brown eyes.

"I'll make breakfast if you take her for a walk," said Byron. "Or I could take her, but she has less of a chance of stealing the Hope Diamond with you."

Connie rolled out of bed. "The Hope Diamond is on display at the National Museum of Natural History. It's a little out of the way."

"Like that would stop her," he said affectionately as he scratched Chestnut's head. "Who's my little kleptomaniac? You are. You are."

"Don't encourage her."

On their walk, a jogger on a stretch break cooed at Chestnut.

"Can I pet your dog?" asked the woman.

Connie reluctantly agreed. Chestnut wasn't going to get better without practice.

"She's so sweet," said the jogger as Chestnut nuzzled closer, wagging her tail. "Does she do any tricks?"

The retriever sat and barked, holding her paw out.

"Isn't that darling? She's very well trained."

"You have no idea," said Connie, pushing Chestnut gently to one side and retrieving the watch she was sitting on. "Is this yours?"

"Oh, thank you. I must have dropped it."

"Must have," said Connie, eyeing Chestnut, who lowered her head and wagged her tail in slow, apologetic circles.

Connie finished up the walk, pausing only to return some jewelry that Chestnut "found" to a woman enjoying the morning on a bench. Back home, Connie found some money tucked in Chestnut's collar.

"You're a bad dog," said Connie.

Chestnut whimpered, but she didn't mean it. Any jog where they returned home with under a hundred dollars' worth of merchandise was progress. Connie stuffed the cash into the Bad Dog jar.

"How much this time?" asked Byron as he put the finishing touches on his signature eggs Bowen, which was basically scrambled eggs with Tabasco and some shredded cheddar sprinkled in. Not her favorite, but he was proud of the recipe, so she played along.

"Twenty-three bucks."

"That's progress." Byron set the plates on the table. He offered Chestnut a piece of bacon. She ate it, then curled up on the kitchen floor, wagging her tail.

Connie grabbed a piece of bacon.

"Hello, beautiful," she said.

"Me, or the bacon?" he asked.

"Don't make me choose." She bit into the strip, tossed half of it to Chestnut. "Not that I mind, but aren't you supposed to be at work?"

"Called in."

"Oh, sick day. Somebody's a bad boy."

"Not that bad," he replied. "Just told them I'd be in late."

"Oh, half day," she said, grabbing a glass of orange juice he'd left on the table for her. "Somebody's a mildly irresponsible boy."

"I'll work late."

Connie blew him a kiss. "You're sexy when you're responsible."

Which was, she noted, always. Her life had been a series of nonstop adventures. Stability was a luxury she'd never had before. Byron brought that to their relationship. The world might be blowing up, but he was always there. She sometimes wondered what he got out of the deal, but she usually told herself to shut up and not worry about it.

He caught her smiling at him.

"What?" he asked.

"Oh, nothing."

Connie resisted the urge to put more pepper on her eggs. She chewed a bite and nodded.

"Perfect. As always."

"So, how was your trip?" he asked.

"Oh, the usual," she replied.

Where once they might've fought over her answer, he knew that she wasn't hiding anything from him. Her adventure in Shangri-la hadn't been especially memorable.

"I did learn the four-point quivering palm strike," she added.

"I thought you already knew that."

"No, I used the five-point version."

"So one less point?" he said.

"You'd think it wouldn't be important until you have to kill a six-hundred-pound ogre with your bare hands," she said.

"Dinner was nice," he said.

She nodded.

"Tia and Hiro are great together," he said. "It's nice when people find each other."

"It is."

Connie paused mid-bite. She knew where this conversation was going. It wasn't as if she was avoiding it, but she wasn't overeager. They'd worked out most of the kinks in their relationship. She didn't want to mess with things.

Byron said, "Did you know, statistically, that when people get married, their friends are more likely to get married?"

And there it was. Unavoidable.

She chewed slowly, wondering what she'd say next.

Sometimes, being a woman of action meant surprising even yourself. Times like this.

"Do you want to get married?" she asked.

He laughed. Nervously. "I wasn't hinting at anything."

"Yes, you were. Although 'hint' might not be the right word."

"Okay, so I've been thinking about it," he said.

"I've been thinking about it," she replied.

"You have?"

She nodded.

"It's not like it matters," he said. "We're together. Sure, there are legal aspects."

"Ooh, legal aspects." Connie leaned closer and kissed him. "You know I love it when you talk about statistics and legal aspects."

"It's just easier to do certain things when you're married. Legally."

"You're talking about the thing."

"Yes. The thing."

They'd talked about the thing off and on for a while now.

"Do you want to do it?" he asked.

"Yes."

He dropped his fork. "Wait. You do? Get married? Or the thing?"

"Both."

He paused, stunned. It was a big deal, another step. She would've been stunned too if it didn't feel right. But it did, and in a life full of chaos, this seemed the opposite of that.

"Are you sure?" he asked.

"Yes."

He processed her answer.

"Are you—"

She kissed him, ran her fingers through his hair. "I'm sure."

He ran out of the room, practically whooping. He was back with a file folder before she managed to take two more bites.

"Adoption isn't easy," he said, "but I've done the research. It'll be easier if we're married." He glanced up from the papers. "So we're getting married?"

"Seems like the sensible thing to do."

He set the file on the table and ran out of the room again. He was halfway out the kitchen when he turned around and kissed her again.

"I love you." His face was a wide dopey grin.

She put her hand on his cheek. "I know."

He left, then returned with a small ring box. "God, I wanted to do this in a cooler way. A romantic dinner. A surprise. I was working on a speech. It's a first draft. I left it somewhere."

"Bedside table drawer," she said.

"You knew? Of course you knew."

"Also, we've talked about it once or twice," said Connie. "It's not as if it's a shocking development at this point."

He set the box on the table and sighed. "I know. I just had this stupid image in my head of how it was supposed to be, but nothing's ever how it's supposed to be with you."

"Sorry about that," she said.

"No, it's fine. It's one of the things I love about you. Not always. Sometimes, it's a little frustrating."

He stopped talking, waiting for her to respond. She didn't. He was so damned cute when he struggled to fill the silence.

"Not that you're frustrating," he said. "You're amazing. You'll be an amazing mom. I'll be an amazing dad. We'll be amazing and have an amazing kid."

"One step at a time, maybe," she said.

"Right, right." He said, "So I've got to go to work, but we'll talk more about it when I get home." He glanced at his watch. "I'm late. Love you."

He gave her a quick peck, grabbed his jacket, and ran out the door.

Chestnut grabbed his briefcase from off the kitchen counter and trotted out of the dining room. Connie heard the front door open again.

"Forgot my . . . Oh, thanks."

She heard the door close again. Chestnut returned to her side, and Connie tossed the dog another piece of bacon.

4

Whenever Connie was home, she'd find the time to make her rounds. Most of the other residents in her condominium complex were regular people living regular lives, but whether through fate or coincidence (or if there even was such a distinction in her life), the building had a noteworthy collection of extraordinary people. They were all just trying to live their lives, like her, but Connie found it often headed off problems to spend a spare a few minutes to check on them.

First up were Luke and Vance, Bluphinite fugitives who lived across the hall. Luke answered the door.

"Hey, fellas," she said. "Just checking on you. Everything cool?"

Behind Luke, Vance was still putting on his face. He tucked the artificial skin under his collar. "Honey, have you seen my right hand anywhere?"

"Last I saw it, it was in the kitchen," called back Luke.

"I looked there." Vance held up his hands, one passing for human, one bright purple. "I can't go out like this."

Luke sighed. "Maybe you should put your hand where it belongs, then."

"Don't start." Vance waved with his purple hand. "Hi, Connie. I'm going to check the bathroom again."

Chuckling, Luke said, "I swear, he'd lose his anterior photospores if they weren't attached to his skull."

Vance shouted from the other room. "I heard that!"

"Everything's fine, Snurkab," said Luke. "Thanks for checking."

"You're welcome. And remember, it's Connie. Just Connie."

"Of course, Connie." But he couldn't resist making the sweeping intergalactic gesture of profound respect. It was a lot of work, and the full affair could take up to three minutes. Fortunately, Luke went with the abbreviated version. She almost walked away, but if he was going to all the trouble, she could wait through the thirty seconds required.

At the elevator, Connie ran into an exceptionally tall woman who radiated a soft glow. She was lean with a supple, muscular grace. She carried two boxes, one in each pair of her four arms.

"Excuse me," she said. "Could you tell me where 5D is?"

Connie pointed down the hall. "Just straight that way. Can't miss it."

The woman nodded as she stepped off the elevator. The doors closed, but Connie would just catch the next one. She pressed the button.

"I'm Connie, 5B."

"I am known by countless names, whispered in hushed reverence by mortals," replied the woman. "For ten thousand years, I have tended the paths of destiny, seeing that which must come to pass and preventing that which must never be. I have witnessed the beautiful things that have never happened and the sorrowful end of all things."

Her glow faded.

"But I'm retired now. That bullshit is someone else's problem."

She set down one box and held out a hand. "Shai Zaya, 5D."

Connie shook the demigoddess's hand. "We're neighbors. You'll like it here."

"I know I will," said Shai with a slight smile. "Your lift is here."

The elevator dinged as the doors opened. Connie stepped inside.

"Nice to meet you."

"You too," said Shai, picking up her box and walking away as the doors closed.

Next on her list was Doctor Malady. On her way down the hall, she passed Jim and Nim. They exchanged some pleasantries about the weather. Nim mentioned a get-together, and Connie promised to check her schedule.

She rang Malady's doorbell, but he didn't answer right away. She rang the bell two more times and was debating kicking it down when it finally opened.

Malady opened the door just enough to stick his head out. "Ah, Connie, so good to see you. What a pleasant surprise."

She nodded. "Hello, Doctor. How are things?"

"Good, good." He wiped a bit of grease off his bald head and adjusted his monocle. "Just managing a few projects."

"Where's the wife?" asked Connie.

Doctor Malady said, "Indisposed at the moment. I'm adding some upgrades."

A static crackle accompanied a flash of blue light in his condominium interior. She could smell something burning.

"One moment, dear Connie."

He shut the door. She listened to his muffled voice, accompanied by a racket of metal hitting metal. Things fell quiet as all the lights in the hall flickered off for a moment. Then the door opened again. Malady was sweating now. Heat poured through the crack.

"All right, Doc," she said. "You know I'm going to have to have a look inside."

"Oh, if only we could, but the place is a mess. And Automatica would never forgive me if you saw it in its current state."

"You know the deal."

"Yes, yes, the deal." He frowned. "I don't suppose you could just take my word for it that I'm not building a doomsday device?"

"It's not that I don't trust you . . ."

She put her hand on the door.

"No, it is that I don't trust you. You're an evil genius."

He held up his hand and shook his finger. "Reformed."

"I'd like to give you the benefit of the doubt, but you did almost blow up the moon once."

"How long will you insist on bringing up that one? It was years ago."

"You threatened to evaporate the world's oceans."

"I never planned on actually doing it. I love the beach."

She appreciated that Malady was mostly reformed, but a reformed evil genius was only one bad day away from building their next killbot. He knew that as well as anyone, which was why he'd asked her to be his evil genius recovery monitor.

She said it slowly this time. "You know the deal."

Malady grumbled. "If you insist . . ."

He stepped aside, opening the door.

Like many masterminds, Malady had a taste for stream-lined simplicity supplemented by a tacky flourish here or there. The design style was Scandinavian, with functionality at the forefront. A couch, a chair, a coffee table, several tasteful rugs on the hardwood floors. Framed schematics hung on the walls. A particle fusion drive sat to one side, humming with a steady rhythm. A tapestry, a keepsake from his mastermind days, was draped across one wall. It depicted a hand reaching down to grab the world. Not the most imaginative design, but Malady wasn't one to waste money on a graphic design team.

"As you can see, Connie, there's nothing to be concerned about here."

He moved the corner of the tapestry to cover the hidden elevator to the secret lab he'd had built under the condominium building. She knew all about it, but she hadn't confronted him yet. He knew she knew, and it wasn't reasonable to expect a mad genius of Malady's caliber not to have a place he could tinker now and then.

He smiled, putting her on edge. She couldn't be sure if that was because she knew something was up or just habit. For most of their encounters, he'd been smiling while doing something threatening the entire world.

Connie pointed to the fusion drive. "I thought we agreed you'd get rid of that."

"Oh, but it's so useful."

Automatica, robot bride of the doctor, stepped into the room. The seven-foot-tall metal woman pivoted toward Connie. The robot smiled, but that was because her unmoving face was cast that way.

"Hello, Connie. Your arrival was anticipated. I am making some tea."

"No, thanks. I'm just doing a quick check. How are those upgrades treating you?"

Automatica said, "My last upgrade was eighteen days, seven hours, nine minutes ago. I am fully functional. Thank you for inquiring."

Malady sidled up to her and folded his arms across his chest. "There is no need to trouble Connie with our affairs. And I am not a child, and I resent being *checked up on* like one."

"You asked me to," said Connie.

"Well, maybe I've changed my mind."

"There, there. There, there." Automatica patted him on

the back exactly four times. "It is for your own good, dear. One must acknowledge one's own failings to move beyond them."

She imitated a laugh with a pair of unconvincing high-pitched chirps. Exactly twice. The second set was a replay of the first. "I'll check the tea." She swiveled and marched into the kitchen.

Connie nodded at the strange collection of parts on the coffee table. "What'cha building there, Doctor?"

"Just some little trifle. Something to keep my boundless intellect busy."

She pointed to a small cube casting off waves of heat as it pulsed with a sickly green glow. "Is this antimatter?"

"Anti-proto-matter, if one is to be completely accurate," he replied sheepishly. "And before you ask, yes, it is stable. Mostly."

"Doc, we have a list of things you can and cannot have. You agreed to it."

"I found it in an old box I was going through. Seems a waste to just get rid of it."

"I'm going to have to take this."

Malady grinned like a malicious clever boy. "Be my guest. But if you touch it with your bare hands, it'll melt the flesh from your bones."

"I will fetch the carrying case," said Automatica as she stepped into the room, carrying a silver tray with a teapot, three cups, and some snickerdoodles.

"Thanks," said Connie.

"I regret giving you free will," grumbled the Doctor.

A cursory inspection of the rest of the condo turned up a pocket nuke, several vials of genetic enhancement serum, a handheld freeze ray, and something round and glowy that Connie found in a shoebox hidden under his bed that she just didn't like the looks of.

"Can I at least keep the freeze ray?" he asked with big puppy-dog eyes. Except that he was always squinting, so it was more like a twitch in his brow. "For home defense."

"Max Jackhammer, Crimebuster, lives just down the hall," she said. "I think you'll be fine."

Automatica lent Connie a box to throw all the mad engineering odds and ends into. Connie went ahead and had a cup of tea, since Automatica had gone to the trouble of making it. Automatica drank none, of course, though she held a cup as she sat at the table. Connie and Automatica chatted about the weather while Malady stared ruefully into the distance. Probably thinking of all those who had wronged him and how he would show them all one day. Old habits, but he was trying.

"Please, do stop by again," said Automatica as Connie left, carrying her boxload of twisted science experiments.

"Yes, do." Malady slammed the door.

She exchanged greetings with Yolanda, the dentist in 2A, and Benjamin, the IT guy in 2G, as they passed each other in the halls. She considered dropping the box off at her place, but the elevator was closer, so she elected to carry it.

The elevator opened, revealing two unfamiliar people. One

was a bruiser in a gray suit. The other was a small woman, also in a gray suit. They both wore sunglasses and had faces warped into permanent scowls.

"Hello," said Connie. "One, please."

The woman, staring straight ahead, pushed the button.

"Visitors or new tenants?" asked Connie.

The large man reached into his jacket, but the woman shook her head. She smiled. Tried to. She must not have had much practice with the expression.

"We're here to see a friend." Her voice was rough and soft. "Azalea Slate."

"I know Azalea. She lives on three."

"I told you we had the wrong floor."

The bruiser shrugged.

The woman's smile dropped. "You a friend of Slate's?"

The bruiser took a step behind Connie.

"Acquaintance. We travel in different circles. Usually."

The woman shook her head at her companion, who moved away from Connie.

"Nice weather we're having," said Connie.

"It's too humid," replied the woman.

The elevator dinged, and Connie paused. Slate was a tough-talking, hard-boiled PI. She handled muscle like this on a regular basis. Probably no reason for Connie to get involved, especially while carrying a box of mostly stable anti-proto-matter.

She exited. "Nice to meet you."

The doors closed on the grimacing thugs.

Her final check of the morning was Duke Warlock in 1B. An unfamiliar woman in heavy white makeup and black lipstick answered his door.

"Hey," she said as she moved her brown bangs out of her eye. "Who're you?"

"I'm a friend of Warlock's."

"Okay. Cool." She stepped away from the door. She was naked, and while she wasn't wearing makeup all over, she was pale enough that it was hard to tell the difference. Her smooth alabaster skin was free of blemishes, aside from a pair of small leathery wings tattooed on her back.

Dozens of flickering electric candles lit Warlock's condo. With the lighting and bricked-up windows, the place was a mix of shadowy dungeon and IKEA modern living. A shimmering fog rolled across the floor. It slipped past the woman, caressing her thigh, and she laughed.

She playfully batted the mist away. "You're bad."

The fog gathered before Connie and congealed into the shape of a tall man in a black cape and teddy-bear pajama bottoms.

"Ah, Connie, so delightful to have you with us." His accent was vaguely European. So vaguely European that at times she doubted it was genuine. "I see you've met Chiroptera."

Chiroptera waved half-heartedly as she slinked into the bedroom. "Warlock, baby, I'll be in the coffin if you need me."

Connie raised an eyebrow.

"She likes the coffin," he said, almost apologetically.

"Kind of low-hanging fruit, isn't she?"

"There are times when the eternal night passes so terribly slowly, when the burden of ages weighs heavy upon these ancient shoulders. In such moments, when the darkness chills even my hollow soul, one finds comfort where one can."

Connie chortled.

Warlock fixed her with his dark bloodshot eyes but couldn't hold the expression more than a moment. He chuckled.

"She's really quite delightful once you get to know her."

"Fling delightful?" asked Connie. "Or vampire bride delightful?"

Warlock paled, which made the blue veins on his face and bare chest especially almost glow. "Oh, no. I already have six ex-wives hounding me through the cursed timeless void. I don't need another."

She didn't bother contradicting him, but Duke Warlock was an old romantic. If he hadn't learned his lesson by now, he probably never would.

He had long ago given up the old-school vampire lifestyle. He'd stopped claiming victims once vampires had become sexy enough that they could just go to the club and pick up a date. It wasn't difficult, but not without risk. Every vampire worried about being seduced by an incognito hunter who might slay them while they were vulnerable. It didn't happen often, but it happened.

"So everything's good here?" she asked.

"Perfectly fine," he said. "Thank you for looking in on me."

"Baby, I'm bored!" called Chiroptera from the other room.

"Yes, Connie was just leaving." Fog swirled around Warlock's feet. "And if you see Baron Solaris, tell him I know it was he who smeared wolfsbane on my doormat. And the affront shall not go unanswered."

Somewhere, thunder cracked loud enough to shake the entire building. A wolf howled.

"Warlock, baby . . . ," called Chiroptera.

"Do lock the door behind you."

As mist, Warlock shot into the bedroom. Chiroptera giggled.

Back at the elevator, Connie ran into Azalea Slate, carrying the unconscious form of the woman in the gray suit across her shoulder.

"If you let me get this box of stuff back to my apartment, I can help you with the big guy," said Connie.

"If you don't mind," said Slate, chewing on her unlit cig-arette as she carried the woman out of the elevator. It was a nonsmoking building. "Think it'll be hot today?"

"Could be," said Connie as the elevator doors closed.

5

It wasn't easy to juggle all the balls in Connie's life. The constant call to adventuring made a relationship complicated at times. But if she was in town (which she often wasn't) and the world wasn't exploding (which it sometimes still insisted on doing), she had a *No Adventures* policy on Saturdays.

Saturdays were for her and Byron.

If aliens invaded or the universe threatened to disintegrate, she'd have to step up. Even then, she'd usually try breaking out her phone first and calling someone else to solve the problem. The perks of a lifetime of adventure were that she knew plenty of people who were capable of handling these problems. It wasn't especially heroic to outsource saving the world, but no one could begrudge her a day off.

It was her turn to make breakfast. She took the easy way out and poured them two bowls of cereal. She went ahead and made some toast, too.

"Oh, medium setting," said Byron, spreading strawberry jelly on his pieces. "My favorite."

"We aim to please," she said. "So I thought maybe we'd stay in today."

Byron smiled. "We stayed in our last Saturday together."

"I thought you liked the staying in."

"I did. I do. But we stayed in the Saturday before that, too." He pulled a small notebook from his pocket and flipped through the pages. "I have some ideas."

"You've been preparing?"

She reached for the notebook, but he pulled it away.

"Ah-ah. It's a surprise."

"I get enough surprises," she said.

"You'll like this."

The birds were singing, and children were playing, and if there were assassins lurking in the shadows, they were good enough at their job that Connie hadn't spotted them. After a while she allowed herself to relax.

Byron's plan for the day had some merit. He'd gone through a dozen review sites and found the most average places to visit. He didn't bother explaining his methodology, but however he researched it, this particular bench in this particular park was the definition of unremarkable. There was a standard-issue playground with standard-issue playground equipment and a standard-issue pond. Children ran around while their parents sat to one side, and an old man fed corn to the ducks. Even the ducks were of average size and color.

"This is remarkably unremarkable," she said.

"I thought you'd like it." He offered her another roasted almond bought from a nearby cart. They were okay.

"See?" he said. "Nothing is blowing up. We're good."

"Uh-huh."

She was fairly certain that the tree across the path was cursed. Although maybe it just had one of those vibes. Not every gnarled tree with a peculiar face-like pattern in its trunk was cursed.

He checked his notepad. "After this, I have us scheduled for an art gallery visit."

"Sure," she said absently, focusing on the possibly cursed tree. It was most likely her imagination, but she thought the two knots in its face glowered back at her.

"Something on your mind?" he asked.

"No, I'm good." She kissed him, leaned into his shoulder. "But let's go before that tree does something I can't ignore."

She pulled him by the hand and led him down the path.

"Evil tree, huh?" he asked.

"Possibly evil tree," she replied. "But that's somebody else's problem today."

The art gallery was small, and the paintings were unexceptional. Mostly landscapes of a few degrees higher quality than might be found in a mid-priced hotel room. To play it safe, Connie avoided looking directly at anything, expecting she'd find a lost painting among the showing or discover a coded secret message. Byron didn't seem all that interested in the art either, but it was nice to just hang out. When he excused himself to go to the bathroom, she sat on a bench, head down, steadfastly minding her own business. She called this Saturday Stance, and it worked well enough.

She checked her phone again. No calls. Unusual, but a good thing. Maybe the universe was cutting her a break today.

She put away her phone and looked at the perfectly ordinary crowd of people gathered at the perfectly ordinary art gallery. And she noticed Jade Nilsson, international thief. Or not. She only saw the woman's profile for a moment, and Nilsson was a master of disguise. But the old woman had Nilsson's striking green eyes, same height. Not suspicious in itself, but how quickly she'd turned away after meeting Connie's gaze was a red flag.

Connie glanced to the bathroom door. If Byron came out right now, she'd ignore it. Nilsson wasn't likely to be planning a heist at this moment. What could be worth stealing here?

She used her phone to contact the secret Interpol site that she had access to. Nilsson had last been seen in Lithuania. The old woman turned a corner, and Connie looked to the bathroom for Byron to save her from a lifetime of adventuring instincts.

Grumbling, she decided to just check. No harm in that. If it turned out she was right, she'd alert security or call the cops or maybe just talk to Nilsson, who would see the wisdom in abandoning whatever shenanigans she might be planning. It'd be nice and easy, and then Connie could get back to her day.

She caught up with the old woman and tapped her on the shoulder. "Excuse me. Sorry to bother you, but do you have the time?"

The woman turned. Up close, there no doubt she wasn't Nilsson. Just a woman enjoying a day at the museum. She glanced at the phone in Connie's hand.

Connie shrugged by way of apology. "Sorry. Forgot I had this."

The woman walked away as Byron appeared beside Connie.

"It's getting to you, isn't it?" he asked. "No call to adventure?"

"What? No." She laughed, put her arm in his. "I'm having a great day with you."

"I didn't say you weren't. But I know you."

"It is weird that there hasn't been at least a phone call," said Connie.

"But is it bad?"

"No, it's not bad. Not necessarily."

"Well, the day is still young," he said, offering her hope. "The universe still has plenty of time to explode."

She loved his optimism. "You're right. So what's next on the agenda?"

—

They met Tia and Hiro at a Chinese restaurant convenient for everyone. It wasn't Connie's first choice. She'd have preferred to have a quiet dinner at home. Although she also thought that when something did happen, it might be better to be out of the condo. Less mess for her to clean up after.

Byron noticed her checking her phone again, but he didn't say anything. He didn't need to. She knew what he was thinking, because she was thinking the same thing. She'd been conditioned for things to go wrong so she could fix them. Even things not going wrong was something she needed to fix.

"This was a great idea," said Tia as Hiro pulled out her chair. "It feels like forever since we just had a nice dinner."

"How are the wedding plans?" asked Byron.

"Oh, fine. Everything is lined up. Looks good."

"Now if you could just talk her into getting on board with the honeymoon," said Hiro.

"You promised not to bring that up," said Tia.

"Did I?" He shrugged. "You can't trust a ninja."

"I thought you were bound by a code of honor," said Tia.

"You're thinking of samurai. And even that was mostly bullshit they sold the peasants."

"Well, don't look at me," said Connie. "I've already told her she didn't need to stick around. I'll be fine for a few weeks un-sidekicked."

"See? I told you," said Hiro. "She's cool with it."

Tia said, "I'm not cool with it. Need I remind you that

when the universe was trying to kill Connie, it was only my intervention that kept that from happening? Mine and Byron's."

"Byron isn't going anywhere. He'll cover for you."

Tia said, "Just what do you think I do for Connie?"

"Okay, okay. Forget I brought it up." Hiro tried flashing his devil-may-care smile. It had gotten him out of many a contentious situation, including once convincing a hungry tiger to turn on its master rather than eating him. But Tia had grown resistant to his charms.

"No. I'm asking. What do you think I do? Just tag along and carry the luggage?"

Connie and Byron focused studiously on their menus.

"I didn't say what you do isn't important," replied Hiro.

"Just unimportant enough that I can take a week off without any consequences," said Tia.

Hiro's face went blank.

"If you vanish on me right now . . . ," said Tia.

"I'm just saying that if it's cool with Connie, maybe you could trust her judgment."

"Oh, you can't trust Connie's judgment," said Tia.

Connie lowered her menu just enough to see over the top but said nothing.

"Connie's sense of danger is skewed, at best," said Tia. "The world could be crumbling around her, and she'd still think she had everything in hand."

"That's because she usually does," mumbled Hiro.

"So you do think I'm just a luggage carrier."

"Hey, anyone want dumplings?" asked Byron a bit louder than was natural. "I could really use some dumplings."

"I support your career," said Tia.

Hiro laughed harshly. "You're always complaining about it." He waved his chopstick in a scolding manner. "Hiro, where did these diamonds come from? Hiro, why did you leave this Fan Kuan sitting on the washing machine?"

"First of all, why would you leave an original Fan Kuan in the laundry room? For a master thief, you could be a little more careful with that stuff. Also, why do you even steal anymore? You're rich."

"It's not about the money," he said. "You should know that."

They turned to their menus. The table sat in awkward silence for a few moments.

"A honeymoon is probably okay," said Byron, testing the waters. "It's been uneventful today."

Tia looked up from her menu. "By whose standards?"

"By anyone's standards," he replied. "Not one thing has happened."

Hiro lowered his own menu. "Wait. Not one incident?"

"Not one," confirmed Byron.

Both Tia and Hiro leaned forward.

"You're joking." Tia said to Connie, "Tell me he's joking."

"He's not," Connie replied.

"Not even a call?" asked Hiro.

Connie pulled out her phone and double-checked. "Not even a call."

"Why didn't you tell us?"

"I didn't want to worry you," said Connie.

"Am I missing something?" asked Byron. "She's had quiet days before."

"That depends on how you measure quiet," said Tia. "It's all relative."

Byron said, "I think you're all overreacting. Like last month. We had that brunch Sunday. Nothing happened then."

Connie hid behind her menu. "Right. Nothing."

"Nothing at all," said Tia from behind her own menu.

Byron gently pulled down Connie's menu. "But I was with you all day. How could something have happened and I didn't notice?"

"It wasn't a big thing," said Connie. "Just a thing with some harpies."

"Only took a few minutes," added Tia. "You were in the restroom at the time."

Byron set his jaw and sighed. "That's how your hair got all messed up. You said it was the wind."

"We were having such a good day," said Connie. "I didn't see the point in bringing up one little harpy attack."

"They were little harpies," said Tia, holding her hands about five inches apart. "Basically angry pigeons with screaming human faces." She shuddered. "You should be glad you missed it."

"Okay, so one little thing happened," he said.

Connie looked away and mumbled into her hand.

He glanced at Tia, who studied her folded hands.

"More than one thing?" he asked.

"I might have averted an alien invasion while you were getting us churros," said Connie, sounding a bit guilty. "It wasn't a big deal. Just a conference call routed from the International Space Station."

"It wasn't much of an invasion," said Tia. "More like a misunderstanding with warships."

"I should have told you," said Connie.

He said, "No, it's not a big deal. Like you said. It's just what you do. Though I do have to ask. How many genuinely uneventful days since we've been together?"

"Uneventful is relative."

Byron shook his head. "That means none. Except today."

"Except today," confirmed Connie.

Tia frowned. "And that can't be good."

Hiro's brow furrowed. "Not good at all. I'm sorry. You're right. We should put the honeymoon off. Just to be safe."

Tia took his hand. "And I'm sorry that I gave you a hard time about stealing."

He kissed her hand. "All is forgiven, my sweet."

"I still am not sure I see what the problem is," said Byron.

"It's a bad vibe," explained Tia. "It's not how things are supposed to work."

A great clatter silenced all conversation. Byron, Tia, and Hiro turned at the sudden noise, expecting to see some armed thugs or a vampire or something, anything, that would demand Connie's attention. All they saw was an embarrassed server and an upturned tray of broken dishes.

Connie hadn't taken her eyes off her menu. "I think I could go for some dumplings."

"Your adventure sense isn't alerting you to anything?" asked Tia.

"I don't have an adventure sense," said Connie.

"Sure you do. You're always spotting things."

"That's experience, not magic. But, no, I'm not spotting anything."

"What about that guy over there?" asked Hiro, gesturing to an occupant a few tables down.

"What about him?" said Connie.

"I don't know. He's dressed in a black suit with a Vandyke. That's kind of suspicious, isn't it?"

Nobody answered.

"Hey, at least I'm trying," said Hiro.

"I'd put my money on that couple over there," said Tia, nodding to a stiff man and woman, eating their meal in perfect mechanical silence. "Could be robots."

"They're not robots," said Connie. "And before you suggest it, the party of five in the corner booth are not vampires. Just pale and attractive. Now can we just enjoy a quiet dinner?"

The server came, and they placed their orders. After she left, Hiro said, "Did you see her ring? Wasn't that the signet of the Shadow Society?"

"Are we really going to do this all night?" asked Byron. "If this is the first uneventful night of Connie's life, can't we simply enjoy it?"

"Thank you." Connie kissed him, and he ignored her checking her cell again.

The meal passed in pleasant small talk. Everyone was on edge. Every loud noise, every customer with the slightest odd trait or the absence of odd traits, was suspect. No one commented on anything, but the sidelong glances and awkward silences were noticeable enough.

Afterward, it was Hiro's suggestion that they go for a walk around the block. It was a chance for adventure to find Connie, though no one expected much. It wasn't the kind of neighborhood where exciting things happened. But she'd found adventure in quieter places, and it was worth a shot.

She walked arm in arm with Byron. By now, she'd stopped checking her cell. She still scanned for trouble, but that took a backseat to enjoying herself. A quiet day could only be a bad thing, but she might as well enjoy it.

A car backfired. Byron and Tia jumped.

Connie patted Byron on the back. "You might as well relax. If it happens, it happens."

"Where's Hiro?" asked Tia. She looked around for him. "That man . . ."

"Sorry," he said, stepping from the shadows. Shadows that were themselves almost unnoticeable in the bright streetlight. "Force of habit. I never lost sight of you."

"My hero." She smacked him on the ass. "You're lucky you're cute."

"Luck has nothing to do with it."

"Did you ever wonder how this cosmic caretaker thing works?" asked Byron.

Connie laughed. "Of course we've thought about how it works. How could we not?"

"I've never really thought about it," said Hiro.

"Well, why would you?" asked Tia, cupping his chin. "No offense, honey, but you're not the introspective type."

"Who's offended?" said Hiro with a smile.

Tia said, "Byron, we've talked about it for hours."

Byron asked, "Then why hasn't it ever come up around me?"

"Because it's an old topic for Tia and me. And we accepted a while ago that there weren't really any good answers."

"Okay, I know that Connie gets dragged into adventures," said Byron, "but how does the universe make that happen?"

"You know how," said Connie. "Stuff just happens to me."

"That ignores a lot of questions."

"Yes, it does."

She recognized that look on his face. She knew the questions. She'd asked them of herself before, but she figured he deserved a crack at them.

"How many bank robberies have you foiled?" asked Byron.

Connie shrugged. "Who counts?"

"A lot, then. And your average person goes their whole life without encountering a single bank robbery."

"This is true," said Tia. Her background in insurance added some gravitas to her agreement.

"So is Connie running across bank robbers or is the universe drawing bank robbers to her?"

"Is there a difference?" asked Tia.

"Maybe." Byron chewed on it a bit more. He'd taken only one course in philosophy in college, and that was a long time ago. "It feels like there's a problem of free will here. Because either Connie or bank robbers or both are being directed to cross paths by some cosmic force. And if the universe is interfering on that level, does it only interfere with Connie? Where does the line exist, and does it exist? If Connie needs to be on the other side of the galaxy in order to keep the universe from exploding, does the universe always find a way to get her there? And if it is aware enough to know that the universe is going to explode and Connie can stop it, then why did it choose to use Connie to stop it? It's the universe. It has to have a near-infinite set of tools to handle any problem."

Connie said, "Like I said. There isn't a great answer."

"And that's okay with you?"

"It has to be okay with me," said Connie. "What other choice do I have?"

"What about us?" asked Byron. "Am I part of your destiny? Are we meant to be together for some grand design? Or am I just an unimportant element of your life that the universe doesn't care about because so far, I haven't gotten in the way?"

"You're never in the way," said Connie.

"But what if some secret agents show up, and they need your help to save the day, and you've got dinner plans with me? Is that allowed? What if the best way to make sure you are where you need to be is for me to have a safe drop on my head so that at my funeral you can be at the right place to stop a zombie uprising?"

"That's grim," said Hiro. "A good question, but grim."

Connie wanted to give him a good answer, but she didn't have one. "Byron, I love you, and not even the universe itself can screw with what we've got. I swear."

It was a big promise, but it did make him feel better, because if anyone could keep it, it would be her.

"Free will is an illusion," said Hiro. "You do what you're going to do, and even if you could decide to do something else, you didn't. So who cares if you could have?"

Tia said, "That's a bit simplistic."

"Is it? Let's talk about Connie and Byron, shall we?"

Connie flashed him a look that said he was treading on dangerous ground, but he pressed onward. He could always vanish in a puff of smoke if things went south.

"Connie, when you met Byron's sister, did you know you were going to end up meeting Byron?"

"No."

"And Byron, when you went to meet your sister, did you know Connie was going to be there?"

"No," said Byron.

"And when you first met, did either of you expect that you would be living together a year later?"

"Of course not," said Byron.

"A whole series of decisions were made by you on that day and every day before that. And even if we ignore all the other decisions made by other people that helped lead you to here, even if we pretend that the only factor that mattered was that day, you have to admit, you didn't know what would happen when you made those decisions."

"That's a bit all or nothing," said Byron. "Either we know how everything is going to turn out or it's all random?"

"I didn't say it was random," said Hiro. "It only appears random because none of us have enough information. Wasn't that the whole deal with the Great Engine? To know everything so that it could control everything? But it didn't know about Connie. And if an ancient omnipotent supercomputer that can see nearly everything can't control its fate, what chance do any of us really have?

"And Connie has been having adventures for decades now, and sure, the caretaker mantle is a driving force behind those adventures. But when it went away, she still ended up having adventures. Because that's who she is. Even when she was having all that bad luck, she still had adventures. Not because she had to, but because she wanted to. Because adventuring is who she is. We are who we are. Our dear Connie is no more or less a victim of the whims of cruel fate than the rest of us. The only real difference is that with her, its machinations are a bit more overt."

"So we just give up?" asked Byron.

"No, we just do our best," said Hiro. "But we accept the limitation that we rarely know for sure what that is."

Tia kissed him. "I'm not sure if that's optimistic or cynical."

"It's both or neither or one or the other," he replied with a wink. "Depends on how well your day is going."

Connie's cell rang. Everyone watched closely as she checked it, only to shake her head and wave them off.

"Hey, Mom. Yeah, I can talk."

"I'm definitely sticking around," said Tia.

6

The next day, Connie dreaded what was to come, but she'd learned that it was best to just get these things over with. She rang Tia's doorbell. Zoey answered.

"Hello, Mrs. Jackson."

Zoey scrunched up her face. "Connie is here!" She walked away as Tia came over.

"You made it."

Connie nodded. "I made it."

"Thank heaven for small miracles," grumbled Zoey. "Thought you'd be on the other side of the world by now."

Connie smiled diplomatically. "Just here to help."

Zoey pointed to a box. "You can start by opening those sake glasses. If that's not too mundane a task for you."

Connie saluted. "Not at all, Mrs. Jackson."

Zoey turned away, rifling through a bag of goodies. "Has anyone seen the almonds? We can't do this without the almonds.

It's bad luck. We're behind schedule and the wedding is tomorrow, and—"

"I'm sure they're somewhere, Mom," said Tia.

"Maybe the world's greatest detective can find them,"
mumbled Zoey.

"Maybe I should leave," whispered Connie.

"Ignore her," said Tia. "She'll be fine once she gets it out
of her system."

"It's not that. It's the other thing."

"What? No adventures still?" asked Tia.

Connie nodded.

"That's no good."

Zoey threw up her hands. "Well, I don't know where those
almonds went to."

"They're in the kitchen," said Connie. "On the counter,
by the refrigerator."

Zoey glared. "Now how would you know that?"

"Because that's where Tia puts things she doesn't want to
lose," said Connie.

Zoey left to check the kitchen.

"She'll be fine," said Tia.

"I should go."

"Oh, no." Tia pulled Connie by the arm. "If something
crazy happens, you'll need me. Either way, you're not leaving
me alone with Mom to stuff wedding favor bags."

Connie gave in. It wasn't a lot to ask.

Zoey returned from the kitchen with a box of almonds. She did not seem happy that Connie was right.

They joined the group gathered in the dining room. All of Tia's friends glanced up at Connie's arrival. It was always odd hanging out with Tia's ordinary friends. It didn't help that the last time, Connie had beaten the shit out of a few of them to save them from being possessed by evil cheese.

"Hi." She waved.

She was greeted with a round of mumbled replies as she took her seat in the assembly line. Millie, who had taken the worst of the beating, sat across from Connie. Connie tried smiling and thought about saying sorry. Again. But if Millie hadn't forgiven her yet, she wasn't likely to today. Connie had even sent apology cards, but maybe the little sad-faced cheese wedge on the card was a poor choice. It'd seemed like a cute idea at the time. But no one left the room, so that was progress.

Tia placed a box of sake glasses beside Connie. "I need you to wrap these and put them in the bags."

"No problem."

Connie started putting sake glasses in bags. She could get through this. For Tia. Then Connie could go back to avoiding Tia's mother and friends, and everything would be right with the world.

Zoey watched Connie wrap every glass, eager for the chance to jump on her for doing it wrong. Small talk floated across the table, but Connie didn't pay much attention. Nobody bothered to try including her.

Tia leaned over to Connie. "We're all really glad you made it."

Everyone else at the table paused. Zoey sighed.

"Why would I miss this?" said Connie.

Zoey sighed. Louder this time.

"These little lantern candleholders are just darling," said Sheila. "Where did you get them?"

"Online. I can give you the website." Tia said to Connie, "I got them because they reminded me of that time we were in Katmandu."

The table quieted. Connie nodded. "Yeah."

Zoey groaned. All heads turned toward her, but no one took the bait.

"I've never been," said Beatrice.

"We recommend it," said Tia. "Thamel is a little touristy, but better than spending a night in a cobra pit, right?"

All eyes turned toward Connie.

"Right," she said.

Everyone chuckled in an awkward but well-meaning way. Zoey smacked the table.

"Oh, that's funny. It's a big joke to you, what you've done to my daughter, isn't it?"

"She hasn't done anything to me, Mom," said Tia.

"The hell she hasn't." Zoey adjusted her ample bosom and squared her shoulders. "And don't sass your mama, young lady."

Her mother's mama act was an affectation. Tia had grown up smack-dab in the suburbs, surrounded by the blandest people to be produced by middle America, and while her mom often claimed to be from the streets, Tia suspected the closest she'd ever been was a Boyz II Men concert that passed through town once. And she'd left early.

"Yes, Mama. I mean, no, Mama. But it's not Connie's fault." Tia held up a gift bag. "Can we get back on track now?"

"It's never her fault, is it?" asked Zoey.

Connie looked skyward and hoped beyond hope for the earth to swallow her.

Zoey said, "Oh, I know, I know. The universe decided Connie was destined for a life of adventure. And it was fine when you were children. None of us had any control over it. If your father and I could have figured out a way of keeping you two apart, we would've. Do you know how stressful it is for a parent to have to worry like that?"

"It all worked out in the end," said Tia.

"Thank goodness." Zoey drew in a deep breath and calmed herself. "But I thought when you both grew up, things would change. I thought Connie would end up running off to God knows where, taking all this craziness with her, and Tia, you'd have a normal life."

"I have. Mostly. What's this about, Mom? You never liked Connie, but you were never this hostile before."

"She's dragging you down. Don't you see it, baby? Look at your life now. Now you're volunteering for these ridiculous adventures? Bad enough when you were yanked into them involuntarily. Now you're going willingly. And what kind of grown woman calls herself a sidekick?"

"It's a good job," said Tia. "And I'm good at it."

"Good at throwing yourself into dangerous situations."

Tia waved her hand and chuckled. "Oh, it's not that dangerous."

Zoey fixed Tia with a cold stare. "Where were you last week? Tuesday?"

"I don't recall," said Tia, though her tone betrayed her guilt.

Zoey held up her phone, having the correct photo at the ready. Tia and Connie posed beside a mass of tentacles and eyes. *Just another day in Dimensions Unknown*, read the caption.

Tia said, "First of all, Zyrothruactholhar the Recondite was a really good guy. Very down-to-earth for a multidimensional god-emperor."

"So you just popped into another dimension to have a nice chat with a space monster, then?"

Tia looked away. "There might have been a thing with a star-devouring creature while we were there. But we were on it."

"Um-hmm." Zoey swiped through a few more photos, but Connie put her hand on the phone.

"You're right. I've made a mess of Tia's life now and then."

Zoey sputtered, losing most of her momentum at the admission.

"No, I made a mess of it," said Tia. "Nobody forced me to be Connie's friend, and this isn't about Connie or my sidekicking. It's Hiro, isn't it?"

Zoey stammered through a few half-mumbled sentences.

"You like Hiro," said Tia.

Zoey smiled, thinking of him. "But he isn't the kind of man I expected you to marry. Connie will back me up on that."

Connie knew a minefield when she saw it. She suddenly wished the conversation was about her again.

Zoey said, "You never would've met him if you hadn't been hanging out with her, doing God knows what."

It wasn't what Connie had in mind. She made a show of checking her phone. "Ooh, look at that. Just got a text from the CIA. I better answer it."

She excused herself as the room fell into silence. She pretended to listen to a voice message as she walked out the front door.

She slumped down on the front porch and looked for something to distract her. Anything.

There wasn't a damn thing.

Tia opened the door and stepped out. She sat beside Connie.

"Sorry about that," said Tia. "You know Mom."

"She's not wrong," said Connie.

"Believe it or not, Connie, the whole world doesn't revolve around your choices. I hate to damage your ego, but I'm an adult. I could have walked away if I wanted to."

"No regrets?" asked Connie.

Tia sucked on her teeth. "Who doesn't have regrets? But at least I can say the ride has been interesting. And she's right about one thing. Without you, I never would've met Hiro."

Connie nodded.

"So it's true?" asked Tia. "You think this is a mistake?"

"What? No, I like Hiro. And I like you two together."

"But . . ."

She should have lied. It wouldn't have been a little white one.

"It's a big commitment, and Hiro hasn't proven the best at that. I know that he's been around for a while, but . . ."

She trailed off, not wanting to finish the sentence, but she'd come this far.

"But this is a big thing. He might not be the best guy to get this serious with."

Tia laughed.

"You don't think I know that? You don't think I've thought about it a hundred times since I proposed? And, yes, I proposed because there was no way in hell Hiro was going to do it. But he said yes, and he hasn't left yet.

"I don't know if it's going to work out or not," said Tia, "but my ex was the most stable guy in the world, and we still ended up divorced. And you of all people should know that life never works out the way you expect. Now come inside with me and let's get these damned gift bags done so I can open a bottle of wine."

Connie chuckled. "You got it."

7

onnie didn't usually suffer from insomnia. The adventure lifestyle meant grabbing sleep whenever you could. She could go for days without sleep, if required, but she could also will herself instantly asleep or awake through meditative techniques she'd learned on Skullox-7, where sleeping for more than five minutes was a good way to wake up in the belly of a hungry tuskbax.

But for the first time in ages, she couldn't sleep. She lay in bed next to slumbering Byron and stared at the ceiling.

Something was wrong.

Something was always wrong, somewhere in the universe.

Her cell sat on the bedside table. She called upon her fabled heroic resolve and didn't check it. She rolled out of bed, shoved the phone into her pajama pocket—just in case—and went to the kitchen for a glass of water. She stood over the sink for a few minutes, feeling on edge.

She went to the window and stared out at the street,

scanning for any sign of trouble. She'd even settle for a mugging to foil.

Chestnut sat beside her, nuzzling her hand. She petted the retriever absently, wondering if the lone gray cloud in the distance was just a cloud or something else. Perhaps a dirigible under a holographic disguise. Maybe a storm elemental preparing to attack the city.

"Can't sleep?" asked Byron.

She'd heard him get up, seen him come up behind her in the reflected glass. "It's fine. Go back to bed. I'll be in in a little bit."

He put his hands on her shoulders. "I can make some warm milk."

"It's fine," she said again.

"I know when it's fine. It's not fine," he said.

She pulled his hands off her shoulders and pulled them around her waist. "I'll work it out."

He asked, "Do you want to tell me what's really wrong?"

She turned away from the window. "Just anxious."

"That's not it," he said. "There's more."

She nodded. "There's more."

She took him by the hand and led him over to the sofa. He sat on one side of her. Chestnut sat on the other, laying her head on Connie's lap.

"I keep thinking about what Hiro said. About how this is who I am."

"I thought you liked who you are."

"I do. But it's a very specific life I live, and it's conditioned me. Look at me. Two days without saving the world, and I'm so on edge that I think clouds are suspicious."

"That's just habit," he said.

"A habit from decades. I don't know if I can change it."

"Who says you have to change it?"

"I don't know. Doesn't feel healthy. And what about us?"

He shook his head. "We're good. I thought we had this all worked out."

"I know we're fine," she said. "But what happens when we get married? What happens when we do the adoption?"

"Is that what's bothering you?"

Connie shrugged. "I don't know. Maybe. What kind of parent will I be when I get an itch to run off into outer space after only twenty-four hours of quiet?"

Byron chuckled, and Connie pulled away.

"No, no." He pulled her back. "I'm not laughing at you. I'm laughing because you're just doing what anyone would do. You're scared about this."

She glowered.

"Maybe 'scared' is the wrong word," he said. "Let's call it worried."

"It sucks," she said.

"Of course it does. But it's normal. This is unusual territory. We're talking about us. About our future. And I know you don't think about that very often."

He was right. A life of adventure usually meant more

immediate problems. It was hectic and often exhausting, but it occupied her time. She didn't spend a lot of time contemplating tomorrow when she was so busy putting out fires today.

"It's okay to have second thoughts," he said.

"I'm not." She took his hand. "Are you?"

"No. Never. I know we can make this work." He brushed her hair aside. "We have so far."

The so far part of that bothered her more than she expected. They'd gone through their trials and tribulations, but the relationship sometimes felt like a barely stable experiment, ready to go critical with one unexpected catalyst.

"We can worry about tomorrow tomorrow," he said. "Anyway, if things keep quiet, we'll have plenty of time to figure out what we're doing."

"That's an awfully big if," she said.

But they all were, in a way. If she hadn't been one of hundreds chosen to inherit the caretaker mantle. If she hadn't been the one to adapt best to it. If she hadn't spent most of her life saving the world. If she hadn't tried to ditch the caretaker mantle. If she hadn't met Byron. If she hadn't regained the caretaker, then almost had it stolen again.

Life was a whole series of ifs, and despite evidence that there were cosmic forces at work, she still wasn't convinced there was any grand plan. But whether it was preordained or merely a series of ifs, she was here. And she wanted to be here.

"You could always enjoy the peace and quiet," he said.

"Sure. That's a good idea." She forced a smile.

"It's driving you crazy still, isn't it?"

"So fucking crazy," she replied. "But I'll be okay. You go back to bed. I'll be in in a bit."

"It's okay. I'm not tired." He ineffectively stifled a yawn as he grabbed the remote. "Let's watch some TV."

Five minutes later, he and Chestnut were asleep. His head resting on her shoulder, he snored right in her ear as Chestnut's head made Connie's lap uncomfortably hot.

And there was nowhere in the universe she'd rather have been.

8

O h, wow," said Byron from the doorway. "You look hideous."
Connie was only halfway into her beige-and-yellow
dress. "You haven't even given it a chance."

"You're right."

He sat on the bed and waited for her to finish with the
garment. She pulled it down and smoothed out the wrinkles,
only to remember that most of the wrinkles weren't there by
accident. Perhaps they were meant to simulate frills, but they
bunched up in all the wrong places and did nothing for her
figure.

Byron helped her with the zipper. "There. All done."

She glanced near the mirror. She didn't need to look into it
and at herself. She'd already tried the dress on a couple of times,
and she knew the terrible truth better than Byron ever could.

"I look hideous."

He hugged her. "You're still beautiful to me."

"Beautiful 'to me' is basically an insult, you realize."

He held up his hands in mock surrender. "I'm not the enemy here. I didn't make you wear that."

Connie said, "Still better than the one Tia made me wear for her first wedding. I think she gets off on it."

He smiled. "It is kind of funny."

"If I could move better in this thing, I'd hit you."

He hid his smile behind his hand, but she could still see that grin in his eyes.

She pushed her way past him. He followed, pausing only long enough to pick up the bright-purple-and-blue corsage in a small see-through plastic case on the bed.

"Almost forgot this," he said.

"Wouldn't want that, would we?" She petted Chestnut, indifferent to a few floating hairs. They could only make the dress look nicer. Chestnut jumped onto the couch and curled up, wagging her tail.

"You look nice," she said to Byron as she undid his tie. He could never get it right. His tux was standard-issue. It was only the bridesmaids who had to look like refugees from a school dance for the terminally color-blind.

"So do you," he said. "You look like my prom date, Annie Guthrie."

"Oh, really." She stepped back and twirled. It wasn't easy to do in the dress, which somehow managed to be restrictive and figure-obscuring at once. "Did you get lucky?"

"She blew me off to make out with Bobby Hoss under the bleachers."

She put her hand on his cheek. "Oh, poor teen Byron. Well, maybe you'll get lucky tonight." She winked. "No promises."

They kissed. He pushed her away.

"We're going to be late."

"We're fine." The windows rattled as a hovercraft appeared beside the condo. Connie opened the window. "I've arranged a ride."

A ramp extended from the craft and Automatica, robot bride of Doctor Malady, greeted them. The Amazonian robot, not being in the wedding party, wore a tasteful blue gown. She extended a hand to help Connie board.

"The Doctor says we should leave now to ensure that he has time to properly prepare his weather control machine."

The sky was overcast, and the venue was outdoors. Malady's weather machine was the main reason Tia had invited him to the wedding in the first place. She was always a step ahead on details like that.

Byron handed their gift to Automatica before climbing out the window.

"Help yourself to a snack," he told Chestnut. "But no pay-per-view." He fixed her with his stern look. "Be a good girl now."

They boarded the craft, and it rocketed away over the city. When it was well out of sight, Chestnut popped into the kitchen, grabbed a couple of dog biscuits, and turned on the TV.

"I don't think she's going to make it," said Zoey.

"She'll be here, Mom." Tia adjusted her crown of flowers.

"I'm just saying she's not here now." Zoey readjusted the crown back to its original position.

"Mom, I do not want to have this conversation." Tia moved her crown. "She'll be here, and if she isn't, then it's because she is off saving the world, so it's no big deal. But she'll be here."

Tia drew in a breath and noted the power of a good push-up bra. Her dress looked great. Did great things for her breasts and made her ass amazing, but it was uncomfortable as hell. After the ceremony, she'd change to something else, tradition be damned.

"You couldn't wear white?" asked Zoey.

"It is white," said Tia.

"It's whitish."

"I'm a thirty-seven-year-old divorcée. I'll wear whatever the hell I want."

She pinned her crown before Zoey could alter it again. Harold opened the door and poked his head in.

"You look beautiful, honey."

"Thanks, Harold."

"Just wanted to tell you that Connie and Byron have arrived with a strange bald man and a robot. Said they'll need ten minutes to set up their weather machine and should be good to go."

He hugged her and kissed her on the cheek. Tia had already been grown when her dad passed. She didn't need Harold to be a father to her, but she appreciated his presence.

He was a good guy, and he could handle her mother most of the time.

He hugged Zoey and planted a big kiss on her. "And shame on you for upstaging your own daughter."

Zoey pretended to disapprove. "Oh, don't be so corny, you old man."

He left, and Tia hoped Zoey would go with him, but she sat in a chair to one side and picked up Tia's bouquet.

They'd elected to have a small affair. Both Hiro and she had agreed that a big to-do was unnecessary. She'd done the big wedding before, and it'd been a fairy tale. It'd also been a shitload of money, and she wasn't the little girl looking for a magical night. An informal afternoon with friends and family (and the family part had been iffy from the get-go) was enough.

"I told you she'd make it," said Tia, instantly regretting it.

"Yes, though you have to admit, it might have been better if she hadn't."

"Don't be silly, Mom. She brought the weather machine."

Outside the window, gray clouds threatened to drizzle over the city.

"What if she ruins things?" asked Zoey. "Like your last wedding. Who can forget that? Your father and I spent a lot of money and those horrible gunmen smashed up the place."

"Okay. First of all, those mobsters didn't ruin the wedding. They ruined the reception. Secondly, they were there looking for one of the caterers under witness protection, not Connie. So that's not really her fault."

"All I know is that these androids, aliens, or wizards show up whenever Connie's around. Don't pretend like it's a coincidence."

"It's not," said Tia. "But Connie has always looked out for me. And, as you have so deftly pointed out, she introduced me to Hiro in the first place."

"Did someone say my name?"

Zoey jumped at Hiro's sudden unexpected presence. Tia wasn't surprised. Not that she'd sensed him, but it was these kinds of moments he lived for. She imagined he'd been lurking unseen for minutes for the opportunity. Sometimes she deliberately set him up so that he'd show himself.

He sat in the chair beside Zoey, holding two drinks in his hand. He cut quite the figure in his formal montsuki haori hakama, though he wasn't wearing the haori overcoat right now.

"Hey, babe," Tia said.

Zoey jumped between them. "It's bad luck for the groom to see the bride before the ceremony."

"Too late now." Hiro set down one of his drinks as he stood and took Zoey's hand. He bowed and kissed it. "And might I say you're looking almost as lovely as your daughter, Zoey."

She tittered. She honestly tittered.

"You're too much." She playfully slapped him on the chest with a schoolgirl smile.

He led her to the door and gestured with a slight bow. "Would you be a dear, Zoey, and make sure everything is in place? I've great faith in the catering staff, but even greater faith in you."

"I suppose a second glance can't hurt things," said Zoey as she left.

"Oh God." Tia slumped in a chair. "My hero."

"Always." He sat beside her and pushed the drink toward her. "Just a little something to take the edge off."

She thought about asking what it was, but she didn't care. They toasted. The liquor burned her throat in a fabulous way.

"You look gorgeous, by the way," he said.

"Damn right I do." She took his hand. "Thanks for noticing."

He raised an eyebrow.

She chuckled. "You look very handsome too."

He ran his fingers along the collar. "Still would've preferred a tux. This thing makes vanishing more difficult."

She raised an eyebrow.

"Not that I plan on vanishing," he said, "but it is nice for a ninja to leave his options open."

"Yeah, well, parents," said Tia. "What are you going to do?"

Connie and Byron opened the door. "Are you two ready for this?"

Tia and Hiro stood. She smoothed his collar as he handed her the bouquet.

"Let's do it," she said.

The reception was on the patio. Connie sat by herself to one side, taking it all in.

Tia approached with two beers and a folding chair. She handed a beer to Connie and had a seat beside her.

"You don't have to do that," said Tia.

"Do what?" asked Connie.

"Be on the lookout for trouble," said Tia. "Everything's fine."

"Better safe than sorry. You look beautiful," said Connie.

"I do, don't I?" Tia stood, then turned around once and curtsied. She'd changed her mind about changing once the ceremony was over. She was uncomfortable, but she looked too good to get out of the dress. Though she had slipped on some sneakers. "And what about Hiro?"

"Hiro always looks great."

"I know, right?"

Hiro, engrossed in a conversation with his parents, winked at her. She blew him a kiss.

Harold came over. "Honey, your mom is wondering when the toasts are happening."

"We told her we weren't bothering with that. It's corny and sappy and it just ends up boring everyone."

"I know, honey, but your mother has her heart set on it." He held up his hands, indicating he was just the messenger.

Sayuri appeared beside Tia. She was as sneaky as Hiro, with actual magical powers to boot.

"I can transform your mother into a cat for a few hours if it would make things easier."

"Appreciate the offer," said Tia. "But I wouldn't want you to go to any trouble for me."

Sayuri nodded. "It's not hard. Just let me know if you change your mind."

She transformed into living smoke and dispersed.

"Sisters-in-law," said Tia with a smile. "She's sweet, really."

Zoey sat at her table, along with Connie's parents. They had grown accustomed to Zoey's moods because they understood exactly where she was coming from. They weren't pleased that Connie was knee-deep in danger either. Zoey liked them. Her mom said something funny, and Zoey slapped the table.

"You should let her give a toast." Connie took a drink of beer. "It'll make her happy."

"You know that she's going to throw in some passive-aggressive stuff about you in there, right?" asked Tia.

"I can take it," said Connie.

Tia sighed. "Okay. Tell her we'll be ready in just a minute, Harold."

He hugged both Tia and Connie, then ran off to deliver the news.

"You did good, kid," said Connie. "You and Hiro are great together."

"Speaking of great couples, what about you and Byron?" asked Tia.

"Oh, no." Connie threw her arm around Tia and led her back to the table. "This is your day. Plenty of time for me and Byron."

Tia joined Hiro and the wedding party at their table, and Connie sat with Byron, who was engaged in small talk with one of Tia's work friends.

Given the go-ahead, Zoey walked to the middle of the

gathering and tapped her glass with her spoon to get everyone's attention. She tapped it a while longer than necessary, just to be sure everyone was looking in her direction. Aside from Doctor Malady, who was adjusting his weather machine to compensate for the clouds gathering around the sunny patch he'd conjured up.

"Thank you all for coming on this special day," said Zoey. "As some of you know, Tia hasn't always had the best luck with weddings. . . ."

She paused, as if expecting a round of laughter. None came. She swept the crowd, but very deliberately didn't pause on Connie.

Zoey opened her mouth to continue, but a bright light flared in the sky above. It burned brighter and larger.

Connie joined Malady, fiddling with his machine. "Something wrong, Doc?"

"It's not my machine's doing," he said.

The object plummeted earthward, directly toward the reception.

"Everyone get clear!" shouted Byron.

The guests dispersed to the edges of the sunny patch as the object crashed into the gift table, crushing food processors and gravy boats and several personalized champagne glass sets. A giant metal egg sat in the crater as its reddened hull cooled.

"What did I tell you?" asked Zoey.

"This isn't her fault, Mom," said Tia.

The egg split into four pieces that fell away to release an alien tripod. The machine extended its legs and stood at its full fifteen-foot height. It scanned the gathering with a single glowing red sensor, then settled its gaze upon Connie. It clomped forward as weaponry sprang from its circular chassis.

"Please accept my apologies for the interruption." The tripod curtsied awkwardly on its three legs. "Constance Verity, for the good of the universe, you must be terminated."

Zoey folded her arms and tilted her head at Tia. "Um-hmm."

Automatica hurled a table, knocking two of the tripod's legs out from under it. It fell over, crashing into the wedding cake.

The tripod attempted to stand, but its pointed feet slipped in frosting. Its flailing limbs nearly took off Malady's head, but Connie tackled him to the ground at the last minute. The limb impaled the weather machine, and the tripod bounced around, trying to shake off the device.

"Your cooperation would be appreciated," said the tripod.

The clouds swirled in dark and ominous patterns as sparks flew from the weather machine.

Automatica leaped upon the tripod's back and sank her fingers into the alien alloy to gain a grip. "Caution is recommended until threat is neutralized, fellow guests."

The tripod hopped and spun, trying ineffectively to dislodge Automatica. It managed to kick loose the weather machine, which crashed in a dented heap at Connie's feet. The crackling device conjured several miniature tornadoes that zipped off in random directions, tossing tables and chairs and decorations with wild abandon.

"This could be a problem," said Malady.

Clouds rolled overhead, covering the reception in a gray twilight. Rain came down in heavy sheets as lightning flashed and thunder rumbled relentlessly. The guests all ran for cover.

"Shut that thing off!" shouted Connie.

"I'll see what I can do, but it shouldn't technically even be working!" yelled back Malady. "Perhaps the quantionic power core was a mistake!"

There would be time enough to lecture him after this was over. "Just do whatever you need to! I've got to help Automatica."

"What's the plan?" asked Tia from behind Connie.

She was soaked. Her dress was probably ruined.

The tripod fired a few wild energy bolts, but its weaponry wasn't designed to fire at anything on top of it. The shots came nowhere near Automatica, but one blew a beautiful tiered fountain into gravel.

Connie pushed Tia down. "No way! I get enough shit from your mom! I'm not getting you killed on your wedding day!"

Lightning bolts shot down from the sky in an odd zigzagging pattern, striking the same three spots repeatedly, conventional wisdom be damned. A whirlwind stripped the masonry from the patio and hurled it at Byron. He saw it coming but lacked the reflexes to do anything about it other than tense up.

The brickwork flung itself past him, improbably missing by inches.

"You need to get out of here!" shouted Connie.

He wasn't likely to have heard her in the howling wind, but he knew what she was saying. He nodded and took a step toward the gazebo.

A lightning bolt struck the ground in front of him. Then to the right of him. Then to the left. A bright blue bolt flashed where he was standing but changed direction at the last moment, arcing toward Connie and Tia. Connie threw herself over Tia, as if it would help. But even her reflexes weren't faster than angry electricity.

Sayuri, sword in hand, appeared beside them. She deflected the electricity with her blade, sending it harmlessly back into the sky. The clouds parted, but the rain continued even with the sun. The howling wind died down enough that shouting wasn't required.

"Are you okay?" asked Sayuri, bits of lightning still dancing on her sword.

Connie and Tia nodded.

Sayuri sprang toward the tripod.

"I guess there are advantages to having a magical ninja sister-in-law," said Tia.

The tripod fired at Sayuri. Rather, it fired at the two dozen phantom images she'd conjured to distract it.

"Help Doc fix his machine," Connie said to Tia as she joined the fray.

The weather machine rattled as fresh clouds roiled overhead.

"Fascinating," said Malady.

"Focus, Doctor," said Tia.

Automatica came flying overhead to land with a thud in the muddy ground. Sayuri danced under the tripod's legs as it struggled to get a good angle of attack on her.

"My dear, would you mind helping me with this? As much as I dislike admitting defeat, it's probably best just to destroy the device," said Malady to Automatica.

"Nothing would improve my happiness index more," replied Automatica as she smashed the weather machine. A blast of hot wind swept outward. The clouds dissolved. The air grew deathly still.

The tripod tripped wildly as it tried to get loose of a tablecloth Connie had thrown over its sensor.

"Uh, is that going to be a problem?" asked Tia of the small glowing orb among the weather machine's guts.

"I imagine it's destabilizing," said Malady. "It would be wise to put some distance—"

Tia scooped up the orb in her dress. It threatened to burn through in seconds.

"Connie, unstable power core!"

She lobbed the core at Connie, who kicked it into the tripod, dead center. The core exploded in a bright green flash, sending clouds of smoke billowing across the venue.

Tia spent a solid minute coughing and rubbing her watering

eyes. Connie and Sayuri stepped from the smoke. Connie held a tiny alien pilot in one hand.

"You must die, Constance Verity," said the alien.

"Your mom is never going to let me live this down," said Connie.

9

While Zoey and Harold struggled to convince the venue management that the incident wasn't their fault, Connie and Tia questioned the alien assassin.

His name was Blog, and outside his tripod, he was eight inches of fluffy green cuteness, with big blue eyes and a long, shaggy tail that whipped back and forth.

"Understand that it is nothing personal," he said as he cradled a coffee mug in his arms and took a sip. "But it's a question of the fate of the universe itself."

"Sure, sure." Connie handed him a shortbread cookie.

"Thank you. You're very gracious. It makes it that much more troubling that I must kill you."

"I can imagine."

He sat on the blackened, torn tablecloth on one of the few tables that hadn't been destroyed in the chaos. Behind them, the manager gesticulated energetically at the broken tripod crumpled beside scorched grass. Connie and Tia focused on the more immediate problem.

Tia had changed out of her gown, electing to just throw it away rather than attempt to salvage it. Hiro had abandoned his ceremonial garb for a polo shirt and slacks. Connie hadn't thought to bring a change of clothes, but Tia had her covered with some jeans and a T-shirt. Even on her wedding day, she was still looking out for Connie.

"Why do you have to kill Connie again?" asked Tia.

"Because Constance Verity will destroy the universe," replied Blog.

"You said that already," said Tia. "But what do you mean by that?"

Blog took a bite of cookie and chewed. "I'm afraid I'm not cleared for that information."

"Right."

"If it was so important that I die," asked Connie, "then why did they send only you?"

"May I have another cookie?"

"Knock yourself out," said Connie.

His tail flicked happily as he grabbed two more cookies, one in each hand, and dunked them into his coffee. He answered her question while chewing.

"It is a truth acknowledged throughout the civilized universe that the Legendary Snurkab has saved the universe from untold disasters. And though it is necessary for her to die now, it would be an unforgivable act, justified as it might be. Whoever kills the Snurkab would forever be shamed. It was too great a burden for most to bear. A lottery was held." He took another sip of coffee and wiped his lips with a napkin. "It's funny. I've never won anything before."

"So what if you failed?" asked Tia.

Blog stood tall and determined. As tall as he could, anyway. "I can't fail. You will die, Constance Verity. Again, I apologize."

"Very considerate," said Connie. "Can you give me one second?"

"Of course." He bowed before helping himself to another cookie.

Connie huddled up with Tia and Hiro.

"What are we going to do with him?" asked Tia.

"He's not really dangerous," said Connie.

"Right now," said Hiro. "But if you let him go, he's just going to come back and try again."

Connie said, "I can't just keep him prisoner."

"Why not?" asked Byron, stepping into the conversation. He was still wearing his suit, though he'd ditched the jacket.

"What do you mean, why not?" asked Connie.

"He's devoted to killing you," said Byron. "Allowing an alien assassin to get more equipment after one failed attempt doesn't seem like a smart move to me."

Connie glanced over at Blog, sitting on the table. He waved at her, and she waved back.

"Doesn't feel right."

"Feels right to me," said Byron forcefully.

Everyone, including him, was surprised by that.

He said, "I'm not comfortable with letting him go. I've learned to live with certain things, Connie. I know your life is full of peril and adventure. But there's a difference between the universe dragging you into adventures and ignoring an obvious threat."

"He's not that threatening," said Connie. "Back me up, Tia."

"Her opinion hardly counts," said Byron. "You've been friends forever. Her perspective is skewed."

"I wouldn't say skewed," argued Tia.

"You ran headfirst into a raging lightning tornado storm less than fifteen minutes ago."

"That's not a big deal."

Byron said nothing, allowing Tia to reconsider her words.

She said, "Oh, shit. That was pretty dangerous, wasn't it? I grabbed an unstable power core too. Oh my God. Mom was right. You are a bad influence."

"Yeah," said Connie. "Sorry about that."

Tia shrugged. "Too late to worry about it now."

Byron said, "I'm not trying to make you feel bad, Connie. We've only been together two years now, but I'm already fairly jaded about this stuff too. It's hard not to be. It's so everyday. Almost mundane. And you handle it well enough. Were any of us really that worried when the alien tripod showed up?"

"It is my thing," said Connie.

"Right. But it's still dangerous, and it's okay to treat this little guy, cute as he might be, as a real threat."

"He's right," said Hiro. "I say we throw the polite little killer into a cat carrier. At least until we get this sorted out."

"I suppose you're right," said Connie.

They broke their huddle. Blog was no longer where they'd left him. He didn't turn up after a cursory search.

"That's terrific," said Byron.

"We'll deal with him later," said Connie.

The ground quaked, and the gazebo, barely holding together, collapsed into a heap of splintered wood. A giant drilling machine burst through the earth, spewing dust into the air. Broken underground pipes sprayed water. The machine rolled forward on its treads to crush a few tables and crumpled gifts. The crunch of fine china and food processors was somehow heard over the rumble of the machine's engine.

Zoey threw up her hands. She cast a defeated glare at Connie as she walked away.

The machine opened, and several nine-foot-tall, four-armed humanoids disembarked.

"Hi, Yars." Connie waved to the others. "This is Yars. He's from the center of the earth. He's cool."

"I thought the center of the earth was a monster," said Tia.

"Some of it is," replied Connie. "It's complicated."

She bowed to Yars, who returned the gesture.

"What's up, buddy?"

Yars drew his sword. The shimmering black steel sang, a

series of repeating notes that had ushered countless foes to the grave. "Our prophets have looked into the sacred stream of Oggurash. They have read the entrails of the dread xyloz beast. They have drunk the poisoned nectar of the blood lotus and whispered in their adumbrative death throes. They have seen, over and over again, that if Constance Verity lives, the universe dies."

Hiro reached for his knockout darts, but Connie made a cutting motion with her hand.

"I don't suppose they told you anything specific, Yars."

"That is not how the visions of the prophets work, as you are well aware."

"Sure." Connie shrugged. "Prophets, right? And they sent you because . . ."

"Your service to the Underrealm is not forgotten. As your greatest friend among its people, I volunteered. No other is as worthy to slay you as I. Know that my blade will sing of your death for a thousand generations. And beyond."

His sword chimed pleasantly as he held it high over his head.

Connie bowed again. "You honor me."

"It is I who am honored," he replied.

He gestured to one of the Underrealmers behind him, who approached Connie, laying a sword at her feet.

"May your death be glorious and bloody," Yars said.

"May your lifeblood satisfy the Hungry Earth," replied Connie, picking up the sword.

"You're really going to duel this guy?" asked Byron.

"Relax. I've got this." She tested the weight of the weapon. "It'll be easier this way."

"Easier? He's huge."

"Oh, sure, but at least this is a one-on-one fight. If I refuse the challenge, he'll come back with a small legion. We don't need that."

She moved her sword in small circles, and it sang its own tune.

"What if you lose?" asked Byron.

She pulled him close and kissed him. "I won't."

She put her finger on his lips. "But if I do, know that I love you."

He'd learned a long time ago to pick his arguments with Connie, and this wasn't one he was going to win.

"Don't lose."

"And let you get out of marrying me?" She winked. "Not a chance."

"What?" asked Tia. "You two are engaged?"

"Oh shit. I'm sorry. I didn't want to step on your big day." Connie surveyed the ruined venue. "Guess it's a bit late for that."

Tia hugged Connie and Byron. "Are you crazy? You just made this day even better. I love you two."

Yars cleared his throat.

"Sorry. Duel to the death to get out of the way." Connie excused herself.

"Congratulations," said Yars, adopting a battle stance.

He nodded to Byron. "Know that our priest kings will mourn your betrothed's loss with a thousand burnt offerings to our savage gods."

"Uh, thanks," said Byron.

Connie's and Yars's steel met in a melodious clang.

10

W e're not keeping that," said Byron, moments after boarding Doctor Malady's hovercraft.

Connie eyed the Styrofoam ice chest holding Yars's severed arm packed in ice. "It would be a dishonor to Yars if I didn't."

"Yars, the guy who just tried to kill you," said Byron.

"He didn't try very hard."

"Funny. From my perspective, it looked like he almost cut your head off three times."

"If he'd really wanted me dead, the fight would've been a lot harder."

"So he only sort of wanted you dead."

She said, "It's an Underrealm thing."

Connie pressed a button on her chair. A small spherical robot rolled out with another martini for her. She placed her empty glass on its tray while taking the fresh drink.

"Thanks."

The robot beeped politely before rolling back down the aisle to its station.

She took a sip. "I don't normally like martinis, but Malady programmed a heck of a recipe into these things."

She settled into her chair. Its massage feature worked a knot out of her shoulder while she scrolled through the music selection. She closed her eyes, listening to Bon Jovi while enjoying comfort humanity was never meant to know. Malady truly was a genius.

"What are you going to do with it?" asked Byron.

"Probably have it preserved and mounted. I'm thinking of hanging it in our bathroom."

"Can I throw a veto at that?"

"We could hang it in the living room. Think of it as a conversation piece."

"Guest bathroom," said Byron. "Final offer."

She shrugged. "Still a little bit of a faux pas, but in the unlikely event Yars ever drops by, we could always move it. Just for the duration of the visit."

"Just in case Yars, the guy who tried to kill you, pops in to borrow a cup of sugar or something."

"One must have a sense of decorum," she replied, sipping her martini.

They enjoyed the rest of the ride in silence. Both of them knew exactly what was going on in Connie's mind. Adventure had found her. The universe was back in order.

The hovercraft let them off at their condo window. Chestnut greeted them, and they each gave her a pet.

"I still think two assassination attempts in a single day is a bit much, even for you," said Byron.

"It's not the record, though usually the assassins had a better reason than 'Just because.'"

She went into the kitchen and found a place in the refrigerator for Yars's arm. It was too big for the crisper, but she managed once she moved a pizza box aside.

"Uh, Connie, did you leave a commando hog-tied behind the couch?" asked Byron from the living room.

She joined him to find a bound and gagged soldier, dressed head to toe in black gear. "That's not mine."

Chestnut barked once, wagging her tail. The soldier glared at the dog.

"I'm not even going to ask," said Byron.

"Watch out for him," Connie told Chestnut, who sat beside him.

"I'm not a child who needs protecting," he said.

Connie pointed to the helpless soldier.

"Okay, point taken," said Byron.

Connie swept the condo for any more intruders. Her search didn't turn up any, but she did find a bomb on the bed. A check confirmed that it was disarmed. She returned, setting the harmless explosive device on the coffee table.

"Good girl," she said. "Someone's earned a treat."

Connie knelt beside the soldier, picked up his rifle, and unloaded it. She pulled away his gag. "Why did you bring a bomb into my home?"

"That's not my bomb," he said.

She didn't see a reason he would bother lying about it. Which meant that someone else had planted it.

"Who sent you?" she asked.

He pushed forth a tough-guy silence. It was hard to take seriously, considering he'd been overpowered by a dog.

She spotted a silhouette moving on the roof of the building across the street. Instincts took over, and she dropped as a shot rang out. The window shattered, and a bullet passed where she'd been standing only moments ago. She fell behind the couch, on top of the commando, as another two shots were taken.

Chestnut knocked Byron to the floor and pulled him by the sleeve to cover behind the TV. The sniper wasn't interested in him, but Connie was glad that Chestnut was there to look out for him. It was one less thing to worry about.

"Okay, this might be a problem," she shouted to him from across the room.

She rolled over low on the floor and reloaded the rifle. She could spray some cover fire, but people lived here. She was working on a better plan when a chill fog swept into the room.

"Excuse me," said Duke Warlock, "but was this troublesome mortal bothering you?"

Connie peeked out. The gothic, vaguely European vampire stood in her living room, holding the sniper in one outstretched arm. It was easy to think of Warlock as a cliché, but he was six and a half feet of ancient undead.

The sniper wore a gray suit. He dangled by his tie, choking and gagging in Warlock's iron grip.

"I was out for my evening constitutional," said Warlock, turning his accent up a few notches, "and I heard quite the commotion. Loud enough to wake the dead."

"Thanks, Warlock," said Connie. "You didn't happen to check if there were any more soldiers out there?"

"This was the only one. Shall I dispose of him for you?" Warlock smiled, baring his fangs at the sniper with a low hiss. It was a touch over the top, but he made it work.

"I need to question him first," said Connie.

"As you wish."

Warlock released his hostage, who dropped limply to the floor on wobbly legs. Connie grabbed the guy by his lapels. "Who sent you?"

The assassin only smiled. "You don't scare me."

She let the guy go. "Warlock, could you maybe . . ." She pointed to her eyes and arched her eyebrows.

"It would be my pleasure."

He stood before the cowering assassin, focusing his hypnotic yellow eyes. "Answer the question."

The hit man answered automatically. "Constance Verity has to die. It has been foreseen."

Connie rolled up his sleeve to reveal a strange tattoo on his forearm. "Well, shit."

"What?" asked Byron.

"It's not important," she replied.

"You're not acting like it's not important."

"Okay, but it's not that big a deal."

"You know saying that makes me think this is a pretty big deal, right?" said Byron.

"He's from an order called the Invisible Scythe. They practice preemptive assassination. It just means that they use precognitive psychics and seers to kill those who would commit crimes against the world."

"Why would they come after you, then?" He turned to the hit man. "Why her? She saves people."

The hit man said, "I don't ask questions. I just get paid to pull the trigger."

"You're part of an order," said Byron. "Don't you have a code?"

"I just go where they tell me to go and shoot who they tell me to shoot."

"Now that you've screwed up, won't they just send someone else?"

The hit man shrugged.

Connie pulled up Agent Ellington's number on her cell. She sent a three-word text:

Cleanup. My place.

The little bubbles danced for a moment before a reply appeared.

I'm having dinner.

Connie watched the bubbles for a few more seconds.

On my way.

"If you won't be needing my assistance any longer," said Duke Warlock, "I shall take my leave. Though I was wondering if I might borrow your assassin for a few moments in the kitchen. I could use a snack."

"Sure," said Connie. "Just don't kill him. And don't make a mess."

"Wouldn't dream of it, my dear." He snapped his fingers, and the hypnotized hit man followed obediently.

She pushed a chair into a corner of the room not visible from the street and sat. There was a feel to her life. Danger didn't usually feel this dangerous. Danger was just background noise. But this was a lot of people trying to kill her. More than normal.

Byron knelt beside her and took her hand. "Hey, you've got this. I'm not worried."

But there was worry in his voice. He couldn't hide it, but he was trying to. For her sake.

She pulled him to her and kissed him.

She looked into his eyes. "You need to go."

11

Byron had called ahead and asked Dana if it was cool for him to stay at her place.

There had been a pause. Longish.

"Of course," she'd answered. "I'll have Willis fix up the guest room."

He'd waited for more. Something smirking, even over the phone.

"See you soon," she'd said, then ended the call without waiting for his response.

He should have gotten a hotel room, but the call had been made. Even if he didn't show up at her door, he'd still have to hear his sister's thoughts. There was no avoiding it once Dana was primed. She meant well, and he told himself that it was because she still saw him as that adopted kid who'd walked in with his thumb in his mouth. She'd always been protective. She also liked telling people when they made mistakes. They were two sides of the same instinct.

He knocked on the apartment door. Willis answered. His long hair was put up in a bun, and he was dressed in saggy flower-print pajamas.

Byron realized he'd been standing on the doorstep not saying anything, and Willis had been standing on the other side of the threshold not saying anything. Willis leaned against the doorjamb, neither smiling nor frowning.

"Hey, man," he said.

"Oh, hi," said Byron.

Willis blinked, absorbing the words at his own leisurely pace. A smile crept across his face, and he nodded to Byron.

"No shit, man."

He pulled Byron in for a tight hug and laughed as he patted Byron hard on the back. He released Byron, bent down, and petted Chestnut.

"I hope it's okay that I brought her," said Byron.

"Dogs are pure souls," said Willis. "Always welcome here."

He grabbed Byron's suitcase.

"I can carry my own luggage," said Byron.

"Nah, man. I got it. Ancient laws of hospitality and all that. Your sister is in the living room." Willis sauntered away to the rhythm of whatever music only he could hear.

Byron paused at the door and employed his disciplining voice.

"Be a good girl," he said. "Please, please."

Chestnut gave him a distinctly unimpressed look before crossing the threshold with her tail wagging. She ran after Willis.

Byron found Dana sitting on the couch, watching TV.

"Hey," he said. "Thanks for letting me stay here."

She glanced up from the TV. "What are sisters for? Plus, Willis loves the wonder dog."

"Yeah, about that . . ."

She waved away his concern. "I've already locked up all the good stuff."

"Cool."

It would delay Chestnut a few hours at least.

Dana said, "Also, I've inventoried. If something turns up missing, we'll just assume your dog took it, and you can pay me back if it isn't recovered."

"That's fair."

He sat on the other end of the couch and waited.

"I'm afraid the guest room is a bit of a mess," she said. "Willis has been using it as his"—she made an air quotes gesture—"positivity space."

"That's okay. I just need a bed."

"It's yours for as long as you need it."

There was another pause that went long enough to become a silence.

"It's nothing serious," he said. "Connie just thought it would be better if I lay low for a while."

"Well, if Connie thinks it would be better . . . ," she replied. He couldn't read her tone.

Willis returned. "Guest room is all set up. If you find any origami cranes I missed, just toss them in the box under the bed."

"Will do."

Byron gave a thumbs-up, and Willis returned the gesture.

He leaned down and kissed the top of Dana's head. "Just realized we're out of flaxseed, babe, so I'm heading to the store. Want anything?"

She reached up and scratched his beard. "If they have any of that soda with the basil seeds in it, I wouldn't say no to a six-pack."

He shoved his feet into some slippers and saluted Byron before shuffling out the door. He took Chestnut with him. It was a relief. One less thing to worry about at the moment. Chestnut might steal a handful of things out in the world, but it wasn't Byron's problem. Not right now.

He excused himself to get a snack. He poked through the cupboards. There was nothing but health food. And not the health food that made an honest effort to taste good, but old-school wheat-germ flakes and unsalted, organically sourced corn chips.

"This is my cupboard," said Dana from behind him. She opened it, produced a bag of Doritos, and held the bag out to him. "Do you want to talk about it?"

This time, her tone was obvious. Sympathy.

"It's complicated," he said. "But things are a bit crazy at the moment."

"Aren't they always crazy with Connie?"

"Crazier than usual. A bunch of people are trying to kill her right now."

Dana bit into a chip with a slight smile and raised eyebrow.

"More people than usual. We both agreed that it'd be smarter if I stepped out of the line of fire."

"Makes sense," said Dana.

He ate a few more chips. He didn't want Dana's opinion, but he wasn't comfortable with its absence. It felt like a doomsday hanging over his head, ready to strike at any moment. Unavoidable. The waiting was the worst part.

"You can say it," said Byron.

"What's that?" she asked.

"That Connie lives a dangerous life. And that I could get hurt. And that we don't really go together."

Dana folded her arms. "Is that what I think?"

"Isn't it?"

"You're an adult, Byron. It's not my job to lecture you. And what makes you think you know what I think? Is that what you expect from me? Just someone to wag my finger at you and tell you you're making mistakes?"

He suddenly felt a bit guilty.

"You're going to do what you want to anyway," she said. "What good would it do either of us?"

"So you do think that?" He felt equal parts vindication and irritation.

She shook her head. "As a matter of fact, no." She flashed a broad smile. "I. Do. Not."

"You don't?"

"Jesus, Byron. You've been with Connie a couple of years now. There had to come a point where I just accepted it."

"There did?"

She laughed. "Oh my God. Did you really come here expecting me to dress you down?"

"No?" He didn't sound convincing, even to himself.

"I'm surprised you didn't just get a hotel room, then." She shoved the bag of chips into his arms.

He dropped the Doritos on the counter and followed her. "I'm sorry. I didn't mean to imply that you were judgmental."

"Oh, I'm judgmental," she said. "But I've had time to get used to the idea of you and Connie. It's your life. It's not my place to yell at you."

She opened a small box on the coffee table and pulled out a joint and a lighter.

"You don't smoke," said Byron.

"Willis doesn't approve of alcohol," she said, lighting the joint and puffing on it. "Compromise is part of relationships."

She offered it to him. He took it in two delicate fingers.

"Jesus, Byron, you're such a narc."

"Didn't you once tell Mom on me when I drank that nonalcoholic beer?"

She stretched back on the couch and closed her eyes. "People change."

He considered the joint. He'd smoked before. Once or twice. Or exactly four times. He knew it wasn't a big deal. But Dana was right. He'd spent his whole life being boring. Hell, he barely drank. It wasn't some profound moral decision. It was just how he'd been living.

He put the joint to his lips and puffed. Coughing, he handed it back to her.

He said, "You have changed."

"And you're still a square."

"I'm not a square," he said, though even he didn't believe it as he said it.

She offered him the joint again. He waved it away and she chuckled.

"What's really bothering you?" she asked. "You wouldn't be so worked up about me judging you if you weren't wrestling with some judgment of your own."

"I'm good," he said.

"Byron, it's okay to verbalize your feelings." She leaned forward and held out her hands in a welcoming gesture. "It's good for your karma."

"I don't think that's how karma is supposed to work."

"Yeah, I'm still unclear on the concept," she admitted. "But I know you. Something's bothering you. And it's not my opinions." She held out the joint. "It could help loosen you up."

He shook his head.

"Connie and I are engaged."

"About time. Congratulations."

He said, "That doesn't bother you?"

"The question is, does it bother you?"

"I think I preferred you as a killjoy."

She curled up in a ball on the coach. "You want my opinion? Fine. I am not always happy about your thing with

Connie. But then I see how she looks at you, even after going to fucking Timbuktu and fighting robot werewolves, after she's done things you and I can't even imagine, and I can tell she really loves you. And you really love her. And that's what matters in the end."

"Even though we're so different?" he asked.

"You're not as different as you think. Not anymore. The people we let into our lives change us. We can't avoid it. If we're lucky, it's for the better. It's like Willis and me. Sure, he's annoying and frustrating and doesn't cut his toenails as much as he should. But he's also really sweet and funny and he's made me a better person. I mean, apparently, I used to be a judgmental ass."

"I didn't say that."

She waved him off. "Not the point."

She sat up and took his hand. "Byron, I love the hell out of you, and if I thought for one minute that Connie was going to deliberately hurt you, I'd fight her myself. I'd lose, of course, because she knows fifteen different styles of kung fu, but that's how much I love you. Nobody fucks with my brother. But you and Connie work. I don't get it, but I don't have to explain it to see it."

"Thanks."

She hugged him, then offered him another hit, which he refused.

"You still haven't answered my question, though," she said. "What's bothering you about the engagement?"

"It's not the engagement," he replied. "I'm really happy about that. But things are getting kind of crazy. Crazier. And now that I'm thinking long-term, I don't know if I can keep up with her."

Dana stared at him in an inscrutable Willis-like manner. She pursed her lips together and made a long, loud farting noise.

"You have been keeping up with her. You may be a square, but you're not the same guy you were when you first started dating."

"But—"

"Damn it. You're really going to make me say it, aren't you?" She closed her eyes and pinched the bridge of her nose. "This is harshing my mellow, so I'm only going to say it once.

"You and Connie go together. And it's always going to be crazy. But that's the package. And don't tell me you don't love it. If Connie broke up with you tomorrow, could you tell me you'd be happy dating someone else? Some regular person with a regular job who doesn't fight robot werewolves?"

"You've already used robot werewolves."

"I'm not great at coming up with examples," she said, "but you're not the boring guy you think you are. Not anymore."

"So I was boring," he said.

"So fucking boring," she replied without hesitation. She burst out laughing, and he couldn't help but join her.

"Willis really has been good for you," he said.

"And Connie's been good for you. Stop worrying about all the bullshit and just accept it. You're in for the long haul."

Byron smiled. "Yes. I guess I am."

He took the joint and puffed on it, coughing and rubbing his watering eyes.

"You're still a fucking square, though," she said with a slight grin.

12

Connie swept up the shards of broken glass while the team of workers replaced her window. She had a standing contract with Les Newsmith's Everything Handy Service. Les's motto was "Anytime, anywhere, reasonable prices, free smiles." She had put that motto to the test, and he'd yet to disappoint.

Within ten minutes of hitting him up via her speed dial, Les and his crew had shown up with a replacement window and gotten to work. His office was located twenty minutes away, but she suspected he always had a van waiting nearby.

Les, a lanky fellow in his trademark red overalls, handed her some paperwork to sign.

"Charge it to the usual account?" he asked with his trademark smile. As advertised, it was a pretty solid smile.

She nodded. "How are the kids?"

"Elvis is in college now."

"Really? Seems like he was just ten yesterday."

"Time flies, eh?" He handed her the receipt. "How are Byron and Chestnut?"

"They're good," she said. "They're staying at his sister's for a while."

Les's smile dropped. "Ain't no trouble between you two, is there?"

"No, we're fine," she said. "Things are just a bit hectic right now."

"Aren't they always? But they'll work themselves out."

His smile returned, and he laughed. Les did good work, but she kept him on call because he had a way of making things seem simpler. At least, more relaxed. He came into her life and fixed things, and after he'd gone, he'd leave some order behind in the chaos.

"You'll handle it," he said, handing her a complimentary lollipop. "You always do."

She especially loved the lollipops.

His team finished up, and aside from the bullet holes in the couch, it would be easy to forget that any of it had happened. But Byron and Chestnut weren't here. And the place seemed emptier without them.

Someone knocked on the door.

Connie cleared her head. She wasn't in the mood for another assassination attempt, but assassins usually didn't knock. She grabbed a sword off the wall, one of the non-cursed ones, just to be safe, and answered.

It was her new neighbor Shai, demigoddess of destiny.

"I hope this isn't an awkward moment. I brought some dessert." She held up a cake on a plate in one pair of hands and a bottle of wine in a third hand.

"You don't bring people housewarming gifts when you're the one moving in," said Connie.

Shai nodded. "Humor me. I haven't met many other people in the building yet and wanted an excuse to come over."

"You aren't here to kill me, are you?" asked Connie.

"Just because you're going to destroy the universe?"

"You know about that?" Connie tightened her grip on her sword. She had a god-killing axe somewhere around here.

"There's very little I don't know," said Shai. "But no, I'm not here to kill you. That wasn't my job even when I had the job, but I'm retired. And if you're wondering whether I'm lying, I can't. Part of being an avatar of fate that stuck with me even after quitting."

"You could be lying about that," said Connie.

"Could be."

Connie weighed her choices. She'd spent most of her life being manipulated by invisible forces, cosmic powers, and vast conspiracies. At least Shai was being honest about what she was.

"Is that German chocolate cake?" asked Connie.

"It is."

"That's my favorite."

"I bought it at the supermarket." She glowered at the cake. "It isn't very good."

"Nice of you to admit."

"Can't lie."

Connie had a short internal debate. She had a contentious relationship with fate, but she could use a piece of cake and a drink.

They cut into the cake in the kitchen. Connie took a bite of her piece.

"You were right. This isn't very good."

"First lesson of fate. You take what you can get." Shai jabbed her fork into her own piece.

"I have to say, you're remarkably chill about me destroying the universe."

The demigoddess held out her glass for a refill of the serviceable wine, which Connie was happy to pour.

Shai said, "Honestly, it sucks. I just retired. I was hoping to get a little relaxation before . . ." She swallowed all the wine in one gulp. "But it is what it is." She grabbed the bottle from Connie and drank directly from it. Shai scowled.

"I should have bought better wine."

"Is this just a coincidence, then?" asked Connie. "I'm about to destroy the universe, and you move into my building."

Shai put her head in her hands. All four of them.

She mumbled, "A woman met Death and then ran from him, only to fall off a cliff or get hit by a car or trip down some stairs or some dumb shit like that. People think destiny or fate or kismet is this precise plan. But it's all coincidences." She spiraled her fork, tapping her plate with a clink. "Coincidences all the way down. It all matters, and none of it matters. Destiny doesn't sweat the details. And that caretaker mantle within you . . . it doesn't either."

"That's a relief," said Connie. "I thought you were going to try to offer guidance or something."

"Not my department anymore. Also, would you listen?"

"Probably not," admitted Connie.

A static discharge filled the kitchen as Bonita Alvarado teleported in. The giant space cockroach twitched her antennae.

"Oh, I'm sorry if I'm interrupting anything."

"No, I was just leaving." Shai stood, pushing away her half-finished plate. "Keep the cake. Or throw it away. Whatever you want. I'm taking the wine, if that's cool."

"Sure."

Shai took Connie by the shoulders. The demigoddess stared deep into Connie's eyes for a long moment as if burrowing into her soul.

"Good luck to you, Connie. I'll show myself out."

The demigoddess offered a curt nod as she passed Bonita.

"Connie, I have grave news," said Bonita. "I know this will come as a shock—"

"I'm going to destroy the universe."

Bonita's antennae fell limp. "You already know?"

"It might have come up once or twice. Who told you?"

Bonita transformed into her human disguise and sat at

the table. "Probability. It's all math. If you know what to look for and how to calculate, you can see every possibility, the likelihood of any event. My people have been studying the caretaker destiny for eons. We understand its influence better than anyone. It's all blindingly obvious. I can show you the equations."

"No, thanks. So far, I've heard that I'm going to destroy the universe, but nobody can tell me how or why. I don't suppose your equations showed you that."

"As a matter of fact, that's why I'm here." Bonita eyed the half-eaten cake. "Are you going to finish that?"

"Be my guest." Connie pulled a beer from her fridge.

Bonita took a bite. "This isn't very good cake."

"Focus," said Connie.

"Sorry. Yes, about the calculations. They're undeniable, but I don't understand everything about them. But they keep pointing to a place on Earth you must go."

"And that's where I destroy the universe?"

"No. Not there. But you must go there."

"Any chance of you telling me why?"

Bonita said, "The math doesn't work like that."

"Of course it doesn't," said Connie.

Bonita wrote down the coordinates and set them on the table. "I have to go run more calculations."

"You do that."

Bonita disappeared, leaving Connie alone in her kitchen with an unremarkable cake.

She held it over the trash. It didn't really matter whether she threw it away. That was where Shai was right. The fate of worlds didn't depend on it.

Connie threw half the cake in the garbage and proceeded to wrap the other in foil. It wasn't thwarting destiny, but it felt like a reasonable compromise.

13

Connie borrowed a Manta Ray, a flying submersible designed by Doctor Malady that resembled its namesake. It was large enough to fit four comfortably. She stopped to pick up Tia.

Tia kissed Hiro good-bye and climbed into the cockpit.

"I can handle this on my own," said Connie as she closed the canopy.

"You're crazy if you think I'm letting you go adventuring alone after yesterday," said Tia.

Connie lifted off. "You only got married yesterday."

"Hiro and I are well past the newlywed stage." Tia waved at him on the street below. "You need me. Oh, hey, is that a mini-fridge?"

Sighing, Connie pushed the yoke and shot off into the sky. The Manta Ray zipped with a pleasant hum of its engines. The acceleration barely registered, and she entered the coordinates Bonita had given her.

Tia poked through the mini-fridge. "Are these drinks for anyone?"

"Help yourself."

Tia opened a water and leaned back in her seat. "So Bonita tells you that there's a prophetic math equation that says you're going to destroy the universe, but you also need to go to this place. And we're just doing it."

Connie said, "It's not like I trust her. I haven't forgotten that she manipulated my life in the past, but she is mostly on top of this stuff. I don't have a lot of other leads, and if there's one thing I know, it's that when in doubt, point myself toward the nearest adventure and let it work itself out."

"Fair enough."

Connie flipped on the autopilot. "I'm really sorry about ruining the wedding."

"Don't be stupid. The wedding went great. The reception got a little messy, but nobody died."

"How do you do that?" asked Connie. "If I was in your shoes, I don't know if I'd keep overlooking stuff like this."

"Sure you would. Because you'd be helping your friend save the world and getting to do cool stuff like ride in a flying submarine. Also, without you, I'd never have met Hiro."

"Still not sure you should be thanking me for that."

Tia narrowed her eyes. "Careful. That's my husband you're talking about."

Connie laughed. "Still sounds weird to hear you say it."

"Still sounds weird to say." Tia smiled at nothing in particular. "Weird, but cool."

"I thought you were past the newlywed stage."

"Maybe not, but you're still stuck with me. And you can admit it. You'd be lost without me."

Connie held out her fist. Tia bumped it.

"So you and Byron, huh?" asked Tia. "It's about damned time."

They passed the rest of the supersonic flight talking about everything and nothing. It was good to catch up.

Somewhere over the Pacific Ocean, the Manta Ray's defense systems pinged as a hovering orb covered in mechanical tentacles descended before them.

"What the hell is that?" asked Tia.

A familiar voice came over the communication system.

"Blessed Snurkab, for the good of the universe, I must now kill you."

"Blog, is that you again?" asked Connie.

The orb ship's many tentacles fired a barrage of deadly disintegrator beams. The Manta Ray dodged aside.

"Nice flying," said Tia.

"Haven't touched anything," said Connie. "It's still on autopilot."

The Ray beeped once, as if slightly annoyed, as it wove effortlessly through the dozens of beams fired by Blog's ship. The Ray looped and barrel-rolled, and inertial dampening systems worked so effortlessly that Tia didn't even spill a drop of her water.

"You are indeed a worthy opponent," said Blog over the communicator as he deployed a hundred seeker drones.

Connie thought about grabbing the controls, but the Ray was on top of things. It veered away, unleashing a barrage of precisely targeted lasers that destroyed the drones in moments.

"Gotta give it to Malady," said Tia. "He knows how to build them."

The Ray swiveled around to come bearing down on Blog's ship. It beeped twice and launched a small missile before Connie could stop it.

"I'd eject if I were you, Blog," she said.

"Your primitive terrestrial technology is no match for the finest—"

The missile struck. The alien orb exploded. Its twisted wreckage fell from the sky.

"Damn," said Tia. "I know he was trying to kill us, but I kind of liked the little guy."

"He'll be back." Connie pointed to a small escape pod rocketing back into space.

"You know, I think we're going to have to figure out some way of dealing with all these assassination attempts," said Tia.

"I think you're right."

A little while later, Connie dove the Manta Ray into the New Hebrides Trench. The navigation computer beeped once, and she swept the lights along the walls. "This should be the spot," said Connie as she fastened the last buckle on her pressure suit.

"I'm guessing it's that big cave," said Tia, wrestling with her helmet until Connie helped her snap it into place. "Is that rubble?"

Connie zoomed in closer with a camera. "Looks like it. Could be remnants of a cave-in. Could be something else. Hang on. I'll take us in."

She gently guided the submersible through the opening, navigating through the path.

"Lucky that it's big enough for us," said Tia.

"Not lucky," said Connie. "Someone cleared this out. Recently. You know how it is. No matter how forbidden or unknown the location, I'm usually either right ahead or right behind someone else looking for it."

She used the submersible's robotic arms to push aside some rubble and went deeper. They emerged into the crumbling remains of the once great cavern and an air pocket. Connie launched a few drones that swept the place with lights. They exited the Manta Ray and scouted on foot. Connie bent down and found some debris bearing stonework markings.

"There was something here, but somebody didn't want anyone finding it."

"Figured that out on your own, did you?" asked the Guardian, stepping into the light. Her spectral body glowed with a soft blue light. The alien ghost sized up Connie and

Tia. "If you're seeking the secrets of the universe, you're a little late."

"We came as soon as we could," said Connie.

"Countless eons in this damned cave, outliving everything I ever knew and loved, out of some stupid sense of duty, and it's all gone. Better luck next time." The Guardian faded into a small orb of light that hovered for a few moments before taking on the appearance of her previous corporeal form.

"Well, this is the topper of a great week. Not even death can free me."

"Maybe you have unfinished business," said Tia.

The Guardian gestured toward the rubble. "The temple is destroyed. The Key is gone. My people forgotten to the ages. I'd say this business is decisively finished."

"If you tell us what happened here," Connie said, "I'll release you."

The Guardian chuckled. "Am I supposed to just trust that you can do that?"

Connie gestured for the alien ghost to lean closer. She whispered something in the Guardian's ear.

"You don't say? But that seems a bit unlikely." The Guardian nodded along. "I suppose it does make some sense, when you think about it."

Connie stopped whispering.

"Oh come on," said the Guardian. "You can't stop there."

"I can."

"Very well, but if I tell you, you promise to finish?"

"You have my word," said Connie.

The Guardian grunted before launching into her speech. Her delivery was rushed and mumbled, eager to get it over with.

"When the universe was still burning in the chaos of its birth, my people had secrets. We saw the signs of countless lesser species and so on and blah blah blah oblivion claims all.

"There was this thing, we called it the Key. We couldn't destroy it, but we could contain it. Built a temple of death around it. Standard trial to test worthiness, hoping someone would come along and figure out what to do with this thing. Then some jerks come along and blow the whole mess up and then take the Key, which I think we can all agree is cheating. But it worked, and here we are. Now, are you going to keep your promise?"

Connie said, "In a minute. Can you describe the jerks in question?"

"Humans, like you. Unremarkable. You all look alike to me, honestly."

"And what was this Key?"

"Its origins are unknown, but there was every indication it was older than this universe. Our attempts to truly understand it were unsuccessful, and we came to believe that it could not be understood, that it actively defied understanding."

"Sounds like a the standard-issue mysterious object of untold power," said Tia.

The Guardian glowered. "There is nothing like the Key.

There will never be anything like the Key. It is a singular thing. Compared to the Key, the Great Engine was but a child's plaything."

"You know about the Engine?" asked Connie.

"In the last days of our fading civilization, we helped a lesser species create it. The Engine was the bulwark against the endless entropic forces emitted by the Key. It was hoped that the Engine would provide balance against the Key, but if the Key is an irresistible force, the Engine isn't an immovable object. It will fail eventually, and woe to this universe—and perhaps every other universe—when it does."

"I think we've got some bad news for you," said Connie. "The Great Engine blew up a couple of years ago."

"The Engine is no more?" The Guardian sat on some rubble, although being a ghost, she didn't sit on it as much as float over it in a seated position.

"Yeah, sorry about that," said Connie.

"You destroyed it? How?"

"Connie destroys stuff like that all the time," said Tia. "It wasn't even her first evil near-omnipotent supercomputer."

"It was the ninth," said Connie.

"I pushed the button on that one," said Tia.

"Do you have any idea what you've done?" said the Guardian.

"It was trying to take over the multiverse. If you build an evil supercomputer, you can't be surprised that someone had to take it out."

"Of course we knew it was a possibility that the Engine

would become malignant. It was deemed a necessary risk. Regardless, it wasn't your place to interfere with things you can't possibly understand."

"Connie carries the caretaker mantle," said Tia. "That's entirely her place."

"The what?" asked the Guardian.

Connie said, "I'm a cosmic lynchpin that keeps the universe from falling apart."

The Guardian stood to her full height and sized up Connie. "You?"

"Somebody has to do it, apparently," said Connie. "I'm just the lucky one with the job at the moment."

The Guardian studied Connie from several angles. "Yes, now I can sense it. Something within you." She cast a sidelong glance at Tia. "Within both of you. A manipulative force."

"That's the caretaker," said Connie. "Some call it a destiny or a calling. I call it a mantle. But whatever it's called, it puts us in the right place at the right time to make a difference."

"Is that what you think? That there's some benevolent guiding power at work?" The Guardian smiled. "How frightfully naive. It strikes me as childishly optimistic to think that a power of such influence would be devoted to making the universe a better place."

"It hasn't always. Some who have had it have used it for evil. Or so I'm told. I think it's neutral. That it's the person who uses it that determines what it does."

"And I'm supposed to believe that you are such a selfless person that you have made it into a force of good?"

"Believe what you want," said Connie. "We're getting off track here."

Tia added, "And if Connie destroyed the Great Engine, it was the right thing to do."

"The arrogance." Anger tinged the Guardian's voice as her spectral glow burned bright red. "You've meddled in forces beyond your ken." The cavern rumbled, and cracks spread across the ceiling.

"I'm going to need you to calm down," said Connie.

"You dare make demands?" The ghost towered over Connie. "My species had conquered the stars before your ancestors crawled from the muck. We set plans in motion. We did what we had to do to ensure that the universe had a chance of continuing. And you think you know better? You dare transgress your place in the grand scheme of things?"

The Guardian's specter howled. A chunk of the cavern crashed down, coming dangerously close to crushing the Manta Ray.

"Uh . . . Connie," said Tia.

Connie punched the Guardian in the gut. The angry spirit's shrieks stopped as she exploded in a cloud of ectoplasm swirling loosely in the air. The cavern calmed.

"You can punch ghosts?" asked Tia.

"It's not so much a punch as a focused direction of chi. A

true master of the technique can obliterate a specter from across the room, but that takes years of study. Who has the time?"

The Guardian congealed back into her humanoid shape. "That hurt."

"Then don't make me do it again."

The Guardian huffed. "Even dead I'm humiliated."

"Tell me what I need to know, and I'll keep my promise to help release you."

The ghost floated to a seat on a boulder. "Fine. Ask your questions."

"You said you built the Engine to counter the Key. What does the Key do?"

"Its purpose, if it even has one, is unknown, but its mere presence amplifies entropy around it. This influence grows the longer it is not contained. Unchecked, it will speed the decay of the universe by merely existing."

"Then why did you hide it here?" asked Tia.

"Not my decision," said the Guardian. "You'd have to ask my supervisors. Oh, wait. You can't. They're all long dead. I suppose it had to go somewhere, and this mudhole was far from galactic civilization, but not so far as to be completely inconvenient. Clues were scattered across the cosmos for those with the right knowledge to rediscover what was hidden. And yet, here we are. Only three groups have ever found this place, and two of them belonged to the pathetic creatures that already live here."

"How would I find the Key?" asked Connie.

"Why bother? The temple was the only thing that could dampen it, and now that that's gone, there's no returning it. It's only a matter of time before its influence destroys everything. There's nothing you or anyone else can do about it."

"Let me worry about that."

The Guardian said, "Any device that could measure space-time decay would do the job, now that the Key is out in the universe. I'd tell you how to build one, but, again, not my department."

"That's okay. I know people."

"That's all I know. Now, are you going to keep your end of the deal or not?"

Connie waved the Guardian over and whispered to her. The ghost's eyes went wide.

"Well, I'll be damned. That's pretty obvious in retrospect."

The Guardian disappeared in a flash.

"What did you tell her?" asked Tia.

"Just the meaning of life," said Connie, walking back to the sub.

"You know the meaning of life?"

"Not all of it," replied Connie. "Maybe about ninety percent of it. Trust me, it's not that interesting. You're better off not knowing."

14

Connie and Tia handed the keys to the Manta Ray to Doctor Malady. He stood halfway out his door and in the hallway. She noticed he was acting a little suspicious. He didn't want her seeing what he was up to in his condo, but she had bigger problems right now. Malady was always suspicious regardless. He had the shifting, sneaky manner of a man who had spent too many hours figuring out how to break the laws of physics with nefarious intent.

He ran his finger along his collar. "The Ray reported some trouble over the Pacific."

"Nothing she couldn't deal with," said Connie. "She handled like a dream, Doc."

He started to duck back into his condo when Connie said, "Hey, Doctor, I know you've just lent me your flying sub, but could I trouble you for one more thing? I wouldn't ask if it wasn't important."

Malady stepped into the hall, closing the door behind him.

"Of course, my dear. I consider helping you in any and every way as penance for the . . . indiscretions of my past."

Luminescent green mist seeped from under Malady's door.

"Are you sure you're not too busy?" asked Connie.

"Oh, that? That's nothing. Though perhaps we should step a few feet this way. It's unlikely that inhaling those fumes would lead to any serious mutations, but why roll the dice?"

They moved farther down the hall. Connie ignored the glowing mist as it discolored the hall carpeting.

"We need a device that can measure space-time decay. You wouldn't happen to have one of those lying around anywhere that I could borrow?"

"Can't say that I do," said Malady, "but I can build one. However, a device that measures entropy would have limited use. It's not hard to find entropy throughout the universe. Everything generates entropy. We, merely having this conversation, generate entropy. The universe is in a constant state of decay. Thermodynamics, and all that."

"Didn't you have a perpetual motion machine at one point?" asked Tia.

He smiled coyly. "The eternitron borrowed energy from a parallel universe, thus skirting the issue. Although it turns out that even that energy would have to be paid back with interest eventually. If I'd left it running another week, the consequences could have been . . . unfortunate."

"How unfortunate?" asked Connie.

"Unnecessary to dwell upon it," he said. "But progress is

never without peril. I suppose I should thank you for destroy-ing it."

"Build this decay-measuring gizmo for me, and we'll call it even," said Connie.

He ran a hand across his smooth head and grinned. "Perhaps a few parameters could be offered. Such as what is the func-tional scanning range of this device?"

"We're not sure," said Tia.

"It's probably still on Earth," said Connie. "Probably."

"While this planet might be a mote of dust on the cosmic scale, it is still a very large place," said Malady.

"If you can't do it, I can always find someone else," she said. "I have Archimedes Lovelace on speed dial, and engineering the impossible is his specialty. It even says so on his business cards."

Malady sneered. "That feckless dunce? His time machine barely even worked." He leaned closer and whispered. "You didn't hear this from me, but his bumbling incompetence means that he technically killed his own father upon first using it. If it wasn't for the temporal anomaly field generator I built for him, he wouldn't even exist anymore. And he doesn't have the decency to send me a Christmas card." Malady's eyes gleamed. "It would serve him right if a terrible vengeance fell upon his head."

"Kind of getting off topic, Doctor," said Connie.

He glanced down at his own tightly wringing hands, as surprised by the sight as anyone. He straightened (as straight-ened as he ever got) and let his hands fall to his sides.

"My apologies, ladies. Old habits. But rest assured this is a task fitting my monumental genius. I shall design, engineer, and construct this detection device for you. I've honestly been seeking a challenge worthy of me."

"How long do you think it'll take?" asked Connie.

"Oh, about an hour. I know it's a bit of a wait, but—"

"That'll work just fine, Doc."

Something exploded inside Malady's condo. He sighed. "It might be an hour and fifteen minutes."

He disappeared behind his door. The stink of burning oil and ozone filtered into the hall.

"Should we be worried about that?" asked Tia.

"I can only spin so many plates at a time," said Connie.

They went back to Connie's condo.

"What if Malady can't build the device?" wondered Tia aloud. "Do we have a plan B?"

"He'll build it," said Connie. "Malady's a genius. The smartest evil genius I know."

"Are you sure about that? You've met a lot of evil geniuses."

"If he says he can do it, he can do it."

"So no plan B?"

"We'll get a plan B when we need a plan B," replied Connie. "For now, we stick to plan A."

"Cool. Cool." Tia nodded. "And what's plan A again?"

"Find the Key. Destroy it. Or, if we can't do that, contain it again."

"And how do we do that?"

"One plate at a time," said Connie.

She sat on the sofa and surveyed her empty condo. It didn't seem like a home without Byron. She'd gotten used to having him around. If things kept up, if they could never fix this problem, then how would she manage a relationship? He'd learned to live with her risking her life, but she couldn't ask him to risk his. Not more than she already did.

Bonita teleported into the room in a flash of light. "You're back," she said. "What did you find?"

Connie recounted her conversation with the Guardian's ghost.

"The Key," said Bonita.

"You've heard of it?" asked Tia.

"Yes, but I didn't think it was real. And I had no idea it was on Earth. Although given the nature of things, I can't say I'm surprised."

She set down a device on the coffee table that projected a three-dimensional rotating math equation. It was all nonsense to Connie and Tia, but Bonita studied it while her antennae twitched thoughtfully.

"This would explain the sudden lowering in entropic decay a few days ago. It very well coincides with the release of the Key."

"Doesn't the Key cause entropy?" asked Tia.

"My theory is that when first released, the Key generated an entropic burst that canceled out other entropic forces."

"Like destructive wave interference?" said Tia.

Bonita and Connie blinked.

"What?" said Tia. "I know some science stuff. Two waves at exactly the right opposite frequencies can cancel each other out."

"A gross oversimplification," said Bonita. "And this is nothing like that, but if it helps you think of it that way, go ahead."

"It's not a coincidence, then," said Tia. "The release of the Key and the quiet day."

Bonita used her hands to manipulate the alien numbers in the projection. "There's definitely a probabilistic entanglement here."

"What's that mean?" asked Tia.

"It means that it's all very intimately connected, though I can't say I understand how."

"I don't get why, if this Key is so important, you sent Connie after it when it was already stolen."

"When the Key was contained, its influence on the universe was minor. It was only when it was released that it registered enough to make it into my calculations. The destruction of the temple must have left a residual—"

"Forget I asked." Tia got up and walked out of the room.

"You must find the Key," said Bonita.

Connie said, "You didn't have to tell me that. I'm already working on it."

"Of course. Meanwhile, I'll be running more calculations."

"You do that."

Bonita teleported away in a flash.

"You'd think she'd be more helpful," said Tia, returning with a drink.

"Where would be the fun in that?" said Connie.

"And we're still not worried about all the people who keep showing up saying you're going to destroy the universe?" asked Tia.

"Except I don't destroy the universe," said Connie. "I keep it from being destroyed. And this isn't the first time I've encountered a prophecy. Or the hundredth. They're not always right. And even when they are right, they tend to be ironic or unexpected."

"So a metaphorical destruction, then?" said Tia.

"Wouldn't that just be the way?" replied Connie.

The condo door flew off its hinges as Automatica burst into the room.

"You could have knocked," said Connie.

The robot bride of Doctor Malady turned her unblinking optical sensors onto Connie. "Constance Verity must die."

"Well, shit," grumbled Connie.

Automatica sprang across the room. Connie slid out of the way as the robot smashed her sofa into splinters with a single punch. Automatica threw another series of punches that Connie dodged easily, having long ago figured out Automatica's fighting algorithm.

Malady came trundling into the room, carrying an awkward-shaped gadget in his arms.

"I don't know what happened," he said between gasping breaths. "I was working on the detection device, and Automatica was helping me with the calculations. She just went crazy."

Connie danced around Automatica's attacks. "Yeah, but maybe you can turn her off before I have to hurt her?"

"I've tried her remote control," he said. "But she seems to have overridden it."

"She can do that?" asked Tia.

"She's a sophisticated learning machine," he replied.

Connie ducked a straight, then barely avoided an uppercut she wasn't expecting. Automatica was adapting.

"No worries, though. I can shut her down with this." He fumbled with the contraption in his hand, trying to hook a final few wires into place.

Automatica clipped Connie's shoulder, throwing her off-balance. The robot almost pulverized Connie's skull with another punch.

Malady pointed his gizmo at her and pressed a button. She stopped moving instantly as smoke drifted from the joints in her neck and shoulders.

Tia said, "We ask you for help, and you send your robot after us."

"She must have seen something in the calculations that I didn't." He smiled with no small amount of pride. "She is a very sophisticated machine."

"Is she going to be all right?" asked Connie.

"I can repair her," he replied. "This device subdues her

without damaging any important systems, but as I don't know the nature of the malfunction, I don't know what would happen when I activate her again."

"Just don't do it while I'm around," said Connie.

"A prudent suggestion."

He reached into his lab coat pocket and withdrew a device the size of an eighties mobile phone.

"I completed your device." He held the tracker out to her.

"Thank you, Doctor." She took the tracker.

"How's it work?" asked Tia.

"Very simply. I hand it to Constance, and two seconds later, it delivers a neurogenic pulse that renders her unconscious."

Connie twitched, then fell over. Malady caught her, though he was not a large man and struggled not to be knocked over himself.

"What the hell, Doctor?" asked Tia.

He awkwardly lowered Connie to the floor, using his free hand to aim a small ray gun at Tia. "Yes, sorry about this. But it really is for the best."

Tia's reflexes kicked in a moment too late as he pulled the trigger. An invisible bolt knocked her out, and she toppled. Malady lunged to catch her, but his reflexes were a bit too late as well, and she ended up smacking the floor.

He checked her head. A small bruise was forming on her cheek.

"Oh well, these things will happen," he said to Automatica, who stood to one side, smiling as always.

15

The doorbell to Dana's apartment rang. Dana and Willis were out, so Byron answered. Nobody was there. He glanced out into the hall. In his old life, he would've blown it off as a prank, but Dana was right. He wasn't the same person he used to be. Mysterious knocks sometimes meant something now.

Satisfied that nobody was lurking, he closed the door and went back to the living room.

Hiro sat on the couch with a can of soda and Chestnut by his feet. He opened it, and ninja training meant that the can didn't so much as make a pop. He held up the can to Byron and nodded.

"Hey, buddy."

Byron rolled with it. "Help yourself. Though I'm surprised you rang before entering."

"I have some basic courtesy." Hiro smiled, a little too pleased with himself, and took a sip of his soda.

"How'd you find me?" asked Byron.

"Finding stuff is part of what I do," said Hiro with a wink. "Not like you were hiding."

"What are you even doing here?"

Hiro balked. "I'm hurt. We're friends. I was just checking on you."

"We're friends?" asked Byron.

"Sure we are."

"I just don't recall us often hanging out one-on-one. Usually it's a Connie and Tia thing."

"That hurts. I consider you one of my closest friends."

"Really? I don't want to be a jerk, but I always thought you resented me. For being with Connie."

"Just because Connie and I had a few on-again, off-again flings? Pshaw. That's the past. I'm a happily married man. Why would I have any reason to be jealous of you? I'm very much in love with my charming and beautiful wife."

Byron chuckled. "I guess it is pretty stupid to think—"

"Idiotic is more like it," said Hiro. "Absurd. Why would I have any problems with you? I'm a handsome, international ninja-slash-thief-slash-man of mystery. Women throw themselves at my feet. Powerful people in darkened rooms whisper my name in dread that I might turn my attentions to their most prized possessions. There is nothing in this world I can't have if I so desire. Well, almost nothing."

He gave Chestnut a pat, and she wagged her tail enthusiastically. Byron suspected she liked Hiro more than she liked him, but it only made sense. They had more in common.

"But Connie has her own mind, and I'm over it," said Hiro. He drifted off, staring into an imaginary horizon.

"Tia's great," said Byron.

Hiro perked up. "She is, isn't she? I love her more than I thought possible. This may surprise you, but some consider me a touch self-centered."

"You?" asked Byron, not even bothering to feign mock sincerity. "I can't imagine."

Hiro poked Byron in the chest. A little harder than was strictly classified as friendly. "See there? That's the sort of good-natured ribbing that marks us as friends. We can call each other out on our bullshit. Point out each other's foibles. Go ahead. Have at me, buddy."

"You can be a bit full of yourself sometimes," said Byron.

"No doubt. Perhaps it's a byproduct of my incredible good looks and vast wealth accumulated via my near-supernatural mastery of the ancient art of the ninja."

"Perhaps."

"Now I'll do you."

Byron held up a hand. "Please, don't."

"You're right. What's there to say about you?" Hiro slapped Byron on the shoulder. "You're so fucking stable and reliable and wonderfully average. Some might call you mundane or banal. Forgettable, even."

"I thought we weren't doing me," said Byron.

"It's a compliment."

"Thanks?"

"Connie and I share too much history for me not to feel something," continued Hiro without pausing. "But Connie and I, we don't work together. We never did. But there are times, when I see you two together, when I just want to punch you in the face."

He laughed. Byron didn't.

"It's not because I want to be with Connie. But you're so . . . you. And of all the people I could have lost out to, it was, well, a thoroughly average Joe like you. But I do like you. I really do. Your existence is a continual reminder of the uninspired drudgery I might have lived if I hadn't been fortunate to be as gifted as I am."

"And we're friends?"

"Perhaps 'friends' is too strong a word. Acquaintances at least. But I'm here because Tia wanted me to check up on you. She said something about things being more complicated than usual. Something about how it's easy to overlook you in the jumble. I told her you were fine. You know the score. You must be used to being overlooked."

His smile dropped.

"She did not like that. And I get it. I love Tia, but five years ago, I would have slept with her and just moved on. I'd tell myself it was the ninja way. No attachments. Nothing to keep me from vanishing if things get cumbersome. But now, I find myself having to ask . . . How are you doing, buddy?"

"I'm good," said Byron.

"Great. Glad I asked. I'll let Tia know." Hiro grabbed

Byron's hand and gave it a quick shake. "Good talk." He held up the empty soda. "Do you recycle?"

Byron took the can and dropped it into the recycling bin in the kitchen. He was unsurprised that Hiro had vanished in the few moments he'd left the room. Chestnut occupied the spot on the couch Hiro had filled. She raised her head toward the door as the bell rang again.

He thought about not answering. If it was Hiro playing more weird ninja games, he could just let himself in. If it was Dana or Willis, they would've just let themselves in. And if it was someone else, Byron wasn't in the mood for visitors.

The bell rang again, and he had to answer it. It wasn't in his nature to let it ring.

He was surprised to find someone was actually there this time. A short, stout woman wearing business casual. She carried a clipboard. Behind her stood a pair of henchagent types, wearing matching suits, matching sunglasses, and matching stoic expressions.

He considered slamming the door in their faces. This was obviously adventure-related shenanigans. Instead, he stood there, staring at the woman, who stared back at him.

"Byron Bowen?" she asked, though the way she asked told him she already knew this.

He nodded. "Can I help you?"

"That is yet to be determined." She reached into her jacket pocket and handed him a business card.

The card read PATTY PERKINS, CONSULTANT.

"What do you consult on?" he asked.

"Oh, this and that." She smoothed her jacket. "May we come in?"

"No." He tried to sound confident, even closing the door a bit. "What's this about?"

Patty adjusted her glasses. He was six inches taller than her, but she radiated this inevitable energy. Like a small boulder that would roll over on you if you tried to push against it.

"It's about Constance Verity," said Patty.

He'd already figured that out.

"She's not here."

Patty smiled, showing she was well aware of this fact. "Our business concerns Constance Verity, but not directly."

"Are you here to kidnap me?" he asked point-blank.

"Probably," she replied.

"You don't know if you're here to kidnap me?"

"May we come in? I don't want to spell it out, but your sister and her boyfriend will be returning home in sixteen minutes, and it would be in everyone's best interests if our business is finished before then."

He wasn't sure if that was a threat or not. It sounded vaguely threatening, and the two agents didn't make it seem friendlier. He thought about slamming the door in their faces, but that was only a delaying tactic. He might have time to get to his phone and call Connie. But if these people were here to abduct him to get Connie's attention, then they'd just call her themselves later.

He stepped back. "Okay, but if this is a kidnapping, can I at least grab a few things before we leave?"

"I'm certain we can make arrangements," said Patty as she entered with her two agents.

Chestnut came over and sat beside Byron.

"I do adore a well-trained dog," said Patty.

Byron said, "How do we do this? I haven't been abducted a lot. Do you want me to call Connie first?"

"Thank you, but unnecessary."

She gestured toward one of her agents, who pulled out a handgun. Chestnut growled.

Byron raised his hands. "There's no need for that. I'll cooperate."

"I appreciate that."

She nodded, and the goon aimed at Byron.

Byron glanced around the room for a weapon. There was a lamp within reach. He could fling it at the agent and then . . . jump behind the sofa or something and then . . .

And then what?

Nothing. He'd do nothing. All the effort would still lead to him being captured or killed. And to highlight the futility, he would already have been shot four or five times by the time he went through all this in his head.

Two darts flashed from nowhere, striking each of the agents in the neck.

"Can't let you do that," said Hiro. "I'm pretty sure my wife would kill me if I let you kill him. And you know what they say. Happy wife, happy life. Plus, I do kind of like the guy."

Patty clicked her pen and wrote something down on her clipboard. "Your interference was calculated, Mr. Yukimura. As was the chemical compound of your knockout darts."

The agents each plucked the darts from their necks with their trademark stoicism.

"Well, that's just not fair," said Hiro as the agents pointed their weapons at him.

Before they could fire, he vanished in a puff of smoke.

"A lot of good he was," said Byron to Chestnut.

The agent stepped forward, aimed, and pulled the trigger. Byron was shocked by it. By the suddenness of it. By the thought that this was how it ended, because that wasn't the way it was supposed to work. By the fact that he was now on the floor and still alive because Chestnut had knocked him down and out of the way.

She jumped in front of him as the agent readied for another shot.

"No need," said Patty, writing something else down.

The agent put away his weapon.

"We'll take them both, but do tell your dog that if she tries any more heroics, I can't promise things will remain civil."

Byron stood, petted Chestnut. "She's a dog. I don't know if she understands that kind of thing."

Patty clicked her pen, tucked it in her pocket. "Oh, she understands."

Chestnut bowed her head and whined.

"Yes, I do adore a well-trained dog. Now, you have exactly three minutes to grab a few things, and then we'll be on our way, Mr. Bowen."

Three minutes later, Byron and Chestnut marched out of the apartment with Patty and her two agents. She closed the door behind her.

Hiro stepped from his hiding place behind a potted plant.

"Tia's going to be pissed," he mumbled.

16

onnie woke in a cell. The windowless, doorless room was tastefully decorated with upper-end IKEA furniture. A surprising number of villains relied on the Swedish furniture company to furnish their holding areas. So much so, that Connie knew the feel of waking up on a Ektorp sofa by feel alone.

She sat up and rubbed her temples, massaging away the slight headache.

Tia lay on the Finnala couch across the Nyboda coffee table. An Underlätta pitcher of ice water, two Pokal glasses, and a plate of macaroons sat on the table. Connie checked on Tia, who was fine, before pouring herself a glass of water.

She surveyed the cell. The stainless-steel walls were mostly bare, aside from a few generic sunset paintings. All very inoffensive in a way that she nonetheless found off-putting. If she'd lived a normal life, this might have been the kind of aesthetic she enjoyed, but given the life she had lived, it felt like a personal hell.

Tia stirred, groaning. "Malady betrayed us."

"I gathered." Connie poured Tia some water and offered her a cookie. "Take this. You'll feel better."

"So much for being reformed." Tia took a bite and frowned. "I'm not crazy about macaroons."

A giant hologram of Doctor Malady's head materialized overhead. It was not the kind of head flattered by being enlarged. "My apologies. I'd have Automatica whip something else up, but, well, you know how my lovely bride is faring at the moment."

Tia said, "I thought you were a good guy now, Doc. Or least not a bad guy. Don't tell me this has all been an elaborate scheme to catch Connie off guard."

Malady frowned. Every exaggerated wrinkle gave the impression of a bag of skin frowning.

"I'm afraid you're misreading my intentions, dear ladies. What I do, I have done out of necessity. I am hoping you'll come to see that."

"This is sounding a lot like the beginning of an evil-genius speech," said Connie.

"Even I can see that, but trust me. All this is merely precaution. When Automatica went rogue, I gleaned that she must have seen something beyond even my staggering intellect."

"Or maybe she just had a glitch," said Tia.

"Unlikely. She is my most sophisticated creation. I must confess that even I don't understand all her learning algorithms anymore. It is my belief, my most fervent hope, that she will one day evolve beyond my genius. Perhaps she already has."

"Always nice to see a supportive husband," mumbled Tia.

"When she went rogue, I thought it best to err on the side of caution. I apologize for the inconvenience, but it was the easiest way to run some tests."

"You could've just asked," said Connie.

"A risk I was unwilling to take. While you were unconscious, I've had my most sophisticated ultracomputers run and rerun the calculations. The common element is that they all keep going mad in the process."

"You're driving computers crazy?" asked Tia.

"For science," said Malady.

"Is this safe?" asked Connie.

"Perfectly," he replied. "I've ensured that each of the computers is a closed system. There was a small kerfuffle when Ultra-6 managed to improvise a basic Wi-Fi connection and attempted to trigger a nuclear strike against this very location. But nothing to worry about, I can assure you.

"Bolstered by my study of this phenomenon, I have discovered a force within Constance. I don't have a better word for it, but it appears to be akin to a localized field of influence. Although its range appears to fluctuate. It defies my complete understanding, but it clearly has an effect on the universe around her."

"It's called the caretaker mantle," said Connie.

"You were already aware of this?"

"It's this ancient magical power that puts me in the right

place at the right time. Also, it helps bend the odds in my favor now and then."

"Intriguing. But could you define 'right place and time' for me?"

"I don't want to get into the mechanics. Partly because I don't understand them myself. I don't think anyone does. All I know is that being caretaker means I get nudged in certain directions by the cosmos."

"And this is the source of your talents, then."

"No," said Connie. "Experience is my talent. The mantle may have thrown me into one adventure after another, but I'm the one who adapted to it. It didn't teach me Martian kung fu or how to dismantle a bomb or fly a Super Cobra helicopter."

Malady's hologram paled. "Yes, yes. I apologize for minimizing your own impressive skills. Regardless, my own measurements of this caretaker force suggest that it is, at least under your possession, a force of ultimate negentropy. Negentropy is entropy's opposite."

"I know what negentropy is, Doc," said Connie.

"So it is that should the Key, an object of ultimate entropy, come into contact with the caretaker mantle, a person of ultimate negentropy, the results would be most likely disastrous. So disastrous that even calculating the mere possibility would be enough to drive ultracomputers to maniacal madness."

"Could it have an effect on prophets and seers as well?" asked Tia.

"That is outside my area of study, but I've long suspected that so-called prognosticators are merely tuned into a probabilistic resonance that most of us are not. I would imagine that such an event would have enough resonance to garner their attention."

"It's all related, then," said Tia. "It has to be."

Malady said, "I do have a solution to this dilemma. We can extract and isolate this caretaker force from Constance. Once she has dealt with the Key in her own reliable manner, I can restore this mantle."

Connie said, "You can take it out of me, Doc?"

"I see no reason why I can't," he replied. "Barring your refusal, of course."

"And if I do refuse?"

Malady's holographic head smiled. There was a natural malignant glee to the expression, but she chalked that up to years of habit.

"Then I have no choice but to let you go."

"You'd do that?" asked Connie.

"I am reformed."

"You knocked us out and threw us in a cell," said Tia.

"I don't suppose an apology would help, but I needed time to study the problem. I thought, better to ask for your forgiveness than your permission. Old habits."

His hologram disappeared as he stepped through a secret door into the cell. "Now that I understand it, I can only offer my assistance."

"We can just walk out?" asked Tia.

"If there's anything my many failures against Constance have taught me, it's that forcing her to do anything would only backfire spectacularly. Foil me once, shame on you. Foil me a dozen times, shame on me. I'll even be happy to give you the entropy detector you asked for." He pulled a chunky plastic cube from his lab coat pocket.

Connie sat on the sofa, thinking.

"And you can give it back?" she finally asked.

Connie and Tia walked down the halls of Malady's secret laboratory. He led the way, along with his worker drones. He had always favored robots over people. Connie was familiar with all his favorite designs. None of the models were of the combat variety. The drones were thin and relatively fragile, not made for fighting.

"You can't really be considering doing this," said Tia.

"He makes a lot of sense," said Connie.

"He's an evil genius."

"Former evil genius," corrected Connie.

Malady, an amused smile on his wrinkled face, glanced back in their direction. He could no doubt hear their hushed conversation, but he made no comment.

" 'Trust' might be too strong a word," said Connie, "but my gut tells me he's onto something."

"But you can't have forgotten last time," said Tia. "The mantle was taken away, and the universe kept trying to kill you."

"That was different. Lady Peril was doing some weird magic thing. It screwed with the rules. And everything worked out because you were there to watch my back, like you are now."

"Okay, but—"

"It's only temporary," said Connie. "Once we handle the Key, it'll all go back to the way it was."

"Yeah, but—"

"Tia, all my life I've been guided by the caretaker mantle. I've been manipulated and controlled. But I'm not just a puppet. I have to believe that I'm more than that. I have to believe that the mantle isn't the only reason I've survived as long as I have."

"Sure, but—"

Connie stopped, grabbed Tia by the shoulders, looked her right in the eye. "We can do this."

Tia had been through a lot with Connie. Alien invasions. Jewel heists. Zombie attacks. Murder mysteries. Rampaging monsters. International intrigue. Earthquakes. Floods. Giant robots. Mob wars. So much craziness it was easy to lose track of it all. But there were moments that stuck out in her memory.

Connie, armed only with a spear, charging a herd of triceratops ghouls.

Connie piloting a barely working spaceship along the event horizon of a black hole.

Connie playing chess with an ancient mountain god to keep him from sinking Asia beneath the sea.

And that was just the stuff Tia had been there for.

But Connie had survived. And she was right. It had to be more than just some magical force that made it possible.

"We can do this," Tia said. Even more surprising, she found she believed it.

Malady gestured toward a sliding door. "This way, ladies, if you would be so kind."

The lab was occupied by a single machine. Worker drones were busy putting the finishing touches on it, connecting a few dangling wires, double-checking calibrations.

"How do you have this?" asked Tia. "You said you just discovered the caretaker force. You couldn't have built it in the time we've been here."

He stood by a panel, studying the readout. "No, it's a modification of something I've been working on: a quantum disentanglement device. Never could get it to work. The theory was that it would sever the quantum field connection of an object, thus separating it from the rest of the fluctuating matter and force fields that make up, as best we can summarize, the existence around us. I thought perhaps it might make said object invulnerable to all physical damage. Or possibly cause a cascading wave unleashing the zero-point energy inert throughout the universe."

"Dangerous things to be experimenting with, Doc," said Connie.

"Duly noted. I only tested it once. On one of my robots."

"Can we see the robot?" asked Tia.

"I'm not really sure where it went. My current conjecture

is that it is either sixteen miles beneath the city of San Diego or possibly projected back to the beginning of our universe with enough potential energy to start the big bang."

"And you want to put Connie in this thing?"

"Oh, I wouldn't worry. This is an entirely different application."

"I'm getting a bad feeling about this," said Tia.

"Exploring the boundaries of knowledge is not without risk," he said.

"It's superscience," said Connie. "You take your chances." She pointed to a chair under an array of crackling antennae shooting electrical current back and forth. "So I just sit here?"

Malady spent a few more minutes checking calculations, making adjustments. The extractor machine started smoking, but he assured them that it was nothing to be concerned about, as worker drones sprayed down the smoking bits with foam. Finally, he took hold of a giant switch on the wall.

"And now, with a flick of this lever, I shall pierce the mysteries of science that hinder lesser minds! I shall teach those fools and simpletons that science is not a simpering beast to be tamed, but a god that bows only before the most brilliant of minds!"

He cackled madly until he noticed that Connie and Tia were in the room.

He adjusted his monocle. "Sorry. Old habits."

"Wait, Doc, maybe this isn't such—" began Connie.

Malady threw the switch. The entire room trembled. Several of the drones exploded in delicate little pops and fell over. Connie burned with a brilliant light. Tia and Malady covered their eyes.

"Fascinating," he said.

Connie felt the extractor's invisible claw wrap around something inside of her. Her entire body itched slightly. Not enough to make her scratch, but enough to make her think about scratching.

Malady went to his readout. "Yes, it's working. It's working!"

A claxon sounded. Several warning lights flashed red.

"That's not right."

Tia took a step toward Connie. Orbs of light prickled Tia as they rose from her skin and floated toward Connie.

"Is this supposed to be happening, Doctor?" asked Tia.

He reached into his lab coat and withdrew a doohickey covered in prongs and buttons. He held the device up to Tia.

"Intriguing. I'm detecting the same caretaker force within you. It must have escaped my initial notice because it was at much lower levels."

"I absorbed some of it a while back," said Tia. "And Byron has a little bit too."

Malady clicked his tongue against his teeth. "Such information might have been good to know, but I should be able to compensate."

Connie grunted through clenched teeth. The extractor was like a raccoon trying to pull an orange through a hole in a fence, too stubborn to let go. And her body was the fence.

"Strange. These readings aren't what I would expect.

Granted, this is all theoretical at this point, but the potential energy stored in this caretaker force is much larger than anticipated. It's as if I've only been detecting the tip of a much more immense pool of dark energy."

Connie tensed. "Any time now, Doc," she muttered as sweat beaded on her brow.

"Wait," he said. "This isn't negentropy. This is—"

A knockout dart flew from nowhere to strike him in the neck. Malady pulled it out as his monocle dropped.

"Oh my."

He collapsed.

"It's okay," said Hiro, appearing behind Tia. "I'm here now."

He moved to embrace her, but she shoved him away.

"You idiot."

Connie's glow brightened, and the extractor groaned and spat sparks.

Tia ran to the giant lever and threw it into the off position. The giant machine wound to a slow halt. Its thrumming died down. The electrical sparks fizzled.

Connie pushed herself to her feet and retched a series of dry heaves.

"What happened?"

"I saved you." Hiro appeared beside her, helping steady her. "You're welcome."

Tia bent down beside Doctor Malady. "What did you do?"

Hiro got that look on his face. The one that said he knew he'd screwed up somewhere, but not how.

"But he was doing a thing to Connie with a giant evil machine."

"He was trying to help us," said Connie, stepping away.

"But . . . secret lab. Weird machine. Mad scientist. What was I supposed to think was happening?"

"Reformed mad scientist," said Tia.

"Okay, so it's no problem," said Hiro. "He's just knocked out. He'll be fine once he wakes up."

The extractor machine sprang to life. Its thrumming sent vibrations through everyone's bones. The worker drones closed in on them. One grabbed for Connie, but she swept its spindly legs out from under it. It crashed to the floor, flailing and squealing helplessly, as the rest moved forward.

"What's with them?" shouted Tia, her voice barely audible above the extractor's screeches and buzzes.

"They must think we're a threat to Malady! Can't imagine why!" Connie shoved a drone. It toppled, knocking over two others. They all squealed and flailed like angry, mechanized infants.

Hiro shrugged. "Fine. The next time I see Connie at the mercy of an evil genius, I'll just assume they're on the same side!"

The extractor exploded. Not all at once. Only a few bits and pieces here and there. A chunk of shrapnel took out several more drones, but reinforcements filed into the room. Half of those tripped over their flailing brethren. The biggest threat was them piling up, blocking the exits.

The extractor radiated heat as it filled the room with smoke.

"We have to get out of here!" said Connie.

Hiro was already gone.

"That man is so aggravating!" said Tia.

"Hey, you married him."

He reappeared behind them. "Sorry! It's a reflex!" He took Tia's hand. "I'll take care of her, Connie!"

Before she could shout a thanks, he and Tia were already out the door. On his own, Hiro would've escaped with ease, but with Tia in tow, it'd be a little more of a challenge.

Connie tried to push her way to Doctor Malady, still sprawled unconscious on the floor. The drones overwhelmed her through sheer numbers. They tugged at her hair and shirt and attempted to wrap their arms around her legs. She threw them off, but there were always more, a never-ending tide of clumsy, stupid automatons pushing her back.

The alarms sounded louder as the extractor machine vibrated and exploded itself to pieces. She had no idea why mad engineering resulted in things exploding, but it was how it always worked.

A security robot stomped itself into the room. Unlike the drones, it was combat ready. It leveled its laser cannon at her. She ducked as it blasted four drones, then clomped forward, crushing several more underfoot.

"I'm trying to help, you stupid robots!"

The security robot grabbed for her with its bone-crushing pincers. She pushed a drone into it, then knocked more aside as she retreated.

The extractor made a long, loud whirring whistle. The

exact kind of long, loud whirring whistle that meant it would explode at any moment. Cursing, she ran from the room. She heard the explosion behind her, felt the heat wash over her. One explosion led to another as she ran down the corridor, pushing drones aside, looking for her escape route. Finally, she spotted the elevator, jumped into it, and stabbed the exit button. The doors swished shut, and she was whooshing upward, while below everything self-destructed.

The elevator opened into Malady's condo. Connie exited the cylinder. A moment later, it plummeted back into the depths. A series of explosions shook the floor and echoed up the shaft. It ended with one final blast, and smoke rolled out of the hole.

"That was a close one," said Hiro.

Tia popped him in the chest. "You idiot. You messed everything up."

"It wasn't his fault," said Connie. "Well, it was, but I probably would've done the same thing if I'd seen it from his position."

"See? Connie knows my heart was in the right place."

"Do you think Malady is dead?" asked Tia.

"I hope not, but we can't wait around for him to show up if he isn't. I just wish we'd gotten the entropy detector."

Hiro held up the detector. "Do you mean this?"

Tia snatched it away. "How did you get that?"

He smiled. "Ninja secrets."

She kissed him. Then popped him in the chest again. "You beautiful, irritating man."

Connie took the detector and turned it on. It beeped steadily. "I think it's working."

"Of course it's working," said Hiro. "I wouldn't steal a broken . . . whatever that is."

"Don't try to charm your way out of this," said Tia. "If you hadn't interfered, well-intentioned or not, none of this would've happened. Why are you even here in the first place?"

Hiro's smile dropped. "Uh, yes, about that. It's Byron. I'm afraid he's been abducted."

He flinched before Tia could smack him.

"It wasn't my fault."

17

Hiro pointed to the office building. "They took him in there."

Tia said, "You followed them all this way and didn't get Byron out?"

"I thought about it. But getting people out is trickier than getting objects. And if something went wrong, if something happened to Byron in the process, I didn't want Connie madder at me than she already would be."

"Smart move," said Connie.

"So what's the plan?" asked Tia.

Connie said, "We go in and talk to them."

"What? Just like that?"

"Just like that."

Connie strolled into the building. She'd considered doing something sneakier. She was no slouch in infiltration herself, but her patience was pretty thin. Sometimes, the direct approach worked best.

As soon as they stepped inside the building, a tactical squad of guards rushed forward to greet them.

Connie held up her hands. "Hi. I'm here to see your boss."

Connie and Tia found themselves in a waiting room with several guards. Hiro had vanished at some point. They assumed he was searching the building for Byron, but while they waited for him to report back, they sat on a couch and enjoyed a fruit and cheese plate.

A short woman in an impeccable suit and an unremarkable man with an immaculate waxed handlebar mustache entered.

"Well, this is a pleasure," said the woman. "I'm Patty Perkins, and this is Reynolds, my right-hand genius. No need to introduce yourselves. We're well acquainted, if only by your remarkable reputations."

"I'm a big fan," Reynolds said. "The way you reversed the polarity on Hercules Herkimer's imperial magnetotron, it was nothing short of inspired."

"You know about that?" said Connie.

"I helped design the magnetotron." He beamed.

Patty said, "Reynolds is my lead scientist and engineering consultant. Perhaps the most brilliant mind on Earth. You can get her autograph later, Reynolds."

"Oh, I wouldn't want to bother her. My autograph book is all the way on the other side of the building."

"I don't do autographs," said Connie.

"Oh." He tried and failed to hide his disappointment. "Well, sure. Why would you?"

Patty dismissed the guards and took a seat across from Connie.

"Just so you know," said Patty. "Our security is a match for even your legendary ninja friend."

"What do you want?" asked Connie.

"To the point. I like that. We want you to bring us the Key."

"I don't have it."

"We're aware of that. But we know you can get it."

"Why do you want it?" asked Tia.

Patty smiled, somewhere between obliging and condescending. "For the same reason you do. To destroy it if possible. Contain it if necessary. We're on the same side."

"But you kidnapped my fiancé to get me to work with you?" said Connie.

"Fiancé? I was unaware. Congratulations. After our business is over, you have to let me know where you're registered.

"My information suggests that you will find the Key. Eventually. And it'd be wonderful if you would trust us, but it's too big a chance to take, given your particular talents and the stakes. Byron is just insurance."

"Makes sense in an evil genius way," said Tia.

"I prefer to think of it as efficient."

Connie said, "Okay. Deal."

Patty's smile dropped. "No follow-up questions?"

"Do they matter?" asked Connie.

"No." Patty folded her hands in her lap. "But we are on the same side, Connie. You'll see."

"I'll believe it when I see it."

"I can respect that."

She held out her hand. Connie didn't shake it.

"Just so you know, Byron matters a hell of a lot to me. And if you do anything that hurts him, well, you haven't seen my talents yet."

"More than fair."

"Now then," said Connie. "Before I do this, I need to see Byron."

Byron and Chestnut were being held in a cell not unlike the cell Doctor Malady had imprisoned Connie and Tia in. It would be very easy to confuse it for a luxury apartment at a glance, aside from the lack of windows and the dozens of guards standing around. The guards were only a precaution for Connie's visit, and she respected that. It wasn't impossible for her to take out a dozen armed soldiers in a room like this, but it wasn't a risk she was willing to take with Byron here.

She hugged him. "Oh, babe, I am so sorry about this."

He chuckled. "This? It's pretty standard, isn't it? I'm just sorry I couldn't figure out a way to avoid it."

"I'm sorry Hiro blew it," she said.

"Don't be too mad at him. He tried his knockout darts. And this is only an inconvenience. They've even agreed to let me call in kidnapped to work and write an abductor's note. Don't know if work will take it, but at least it's something."

"I'll get you out of here," she said.

"I know you will. I love you."

"I love you, too."

She hugged him again, then knelt down to let Chestnut lick her face.

"And you, take care of him."

Chestnut raised a paw to her temple in a salute.

The guards ringed Connie as she left the cell, glancing over her shoulder to see Byron wave before the sliding door swished shut with a loud locking click.

Patty said, "Everything will be fine. Let me see you out. I trust your ninja friend will find his own way out."

She escorted them from the premises. On the way, they passed a band of commandoes captured by Patty's forces.

She said, "I hope you don't mind, but I took the liberty of intercepting some assassins that were lying in wait for you outside. No need to thank me."

On the street, they were joined by Hiro.

"Well?" asked Connie.

"Place is locked up tight," he replied. "I could get in and out on my own all day, but with Byron . . . not going to happen."

She wasn't surprised.

"What now?" asked Tia, as if she didn't already know.

"We get the Key. We rescue Byron," said Connie. "We save the world, maybe the universe."

A shot rang out. A sniper fell off a building across the street, hitting the pavement with a thud.

"Oh, sorry about that," said Patty, standing beside her own sharpshooter. "Must have missed one."

Patty watched Connie drive away on a security monitor.

"Why did we steal the Key just to give it to Ajaw Cassowary if we're going to send Verity after it?" asked Reynolds.

"Cassowary paid for our expedition to claim the Key," she replied. "It would be unethical not to give it to him. Professionals must have standards."

"We could've just told her where to find it."

"Please. If she's as good as she's supposed to be, she'll find it on her own. And it will buy us enough time to run your experiments."

His mustache twitched, as it often did when he was exploring the bounds of an interesting scientific experiment.

"Our initial readings suggest it's best to start at a low threat level."

"You know your business. Do what you think is best, Reynolds."

He clicked his heels together and left. She didn't know why he did that, but genius of his caliber meant ignoring quirks.

She studied Byron on another monitor. He sat, petting his dog, every bit oblivious to the fate in store for him.

18

On the way home, a robot from the future tried to kill Connie. It didn't succeed, but it did end up wrecking her car. Something clearly had to be done about these assassins if she was going to get anything accomplished

Shai Zaya answered the door before Connie knocked.

"Please, come in." Shai made a sweeping, welcoming gesture. "You were expected."

Connie stepped across the threshold, but Shai held up her hand when Tia and Hiro attempted to enter.

"I'm afraid you'll need to stay out there. Won't be a moment."

She closed the door on them before they could protest. Although there was little point in protesting Shai or the forces she represented.

"I assume you know why I'm here," said Connie.

"There is very little I don't know," replied Shai. "You seek to cloak yourself from the all-seeing eye of destiny."

She paused just long enough to make Connie think she should say something.

"Yes, it's possible to do so," said Shai.

She smiled enigmatically. Connie opened her mouth to speak.

"Yes, I'll help you," said Shai. The beautiful demigoddess glided past Connie and gestured toward a recliner. "Please, sit."

"I'm kind of in a hurry," said Connie.

Shai sat in her own recliner and folded her hands across her lap. "It doesn't matter how quickly you scramble toward your destiny. It will come at its own time. Not before." She focused her deep brown eyes on Connie. The demigoddess's smile dropped.

This was why Connie avoided anthropomorphic personifications of fate. They always acted as if they knew more than you, and they did. But they also loved teasing and hinting and offering obscure hints of what was to come.

Shai gestured toward the recliner again.

"I'll stand," said Connie, feeling defiant.

Shai's smile returned. "Of course you will."

"What if I'd chosen to sit?" asked Connie.

"You'd be more comfortable, but the conversation would play out the same," said Shai. "Mortals think it all matters, but the truth is that most of it doesn't. The devil isn't in the details. The universe doesn't give a damn if you sit or stand. But if it makes you feel better to stand, I'm not going to argue."

With a sigh of acceptance, Connie sat.

"For ten thousand years, I've guarded the mysteries of fate," said Shai. "And yet, this moment has come. You're never quite ready for it."

"So it's certain, then. I'm going to destroy the universe."

"It will come to pass, yes."

"And there's no way to stop it?"

"I have seen the way of it all. I'm not here to tell you how to stop it."

"But it can be stopped?"

Shai shrugged. She opened a simple carved box on her table and removed a circle of plain thread.

"You want this."

She held it out to Connie.

"I just wear it?"

"That's all it takes. But, just to be clear, the Strand of Hemsut doesn't change what will happen. It just makes it so that those who see such things won't notice you anymore."

"Good enough."

Connie wrapped the strand around her wrist. It disappeared, though she could still feel it.

Shai exhaled and rubbed her temples. "Thank gods. You have no idea how much of a headache you were giving me. Like looking straight into the sun. And now is the part where you tell me you don't believe in destiny."

"I thought you couldn't read me anymore?"

"I can't, but it's the obvious thing. I've had this argument so many times before. As if gumption and good intentions were enough to counter grand cosmic forces. Now if you'll excuse me, I'd like to enjoy the remaining time the universe has left."

"I've countered grand cosmic forces before," said Connie as she exited the apartment.

Shai smiled again. "Everyone's luck runs out eventually. Even yours."

The goddess closed the door with a quiet, definitive click.

19

The door to Byron's cell opened. He sat up on the couch, expecting to see someone.

Chestnut jumped up and ran out. She returned a moment later. She barked, wagging her tail.

"We should probably wait for Connie to rescue us."

The dog fixed him with a disappointed stare. She turned toward the open door and barked again.

Byron studied the open door. Surely it would close again. Or an alarm would sound any minute now.

Chestnut walked back and forth before the exit and whined. Byron had never had his courage challenged by a dog. It didn't feel great.

"Oh my God, this is stupid. You don't know what I'm saying. You're not judging me."

He knelt down. She came over and nuzzled his hands. Then took his sleeve in her mouth and gently pulled him toward escape.

He couldn't take it. Chestnut might not be judging him. She might only be doing what she was trained to do, but it wasn't out of the question that she might be able to get him out of here.

The door was still open. There wasn't a trace of a guard or alarm. He could follow a dog to freedom or get himself killed. Or he could sit here, staring at the exit, like a cowardly lab rat.

Any outcome would make him feel dumb.

Chestnut put her paw on his hand and looked up at him with her big brown eyes.

"Okay, but for the record, I think this is a bad idea."

She barked, licked his cheek before hopping eagerly toward the exit. He followed her out, where there were no guards. Just a hallway that looked so painfully generic he thought he must have been dreaming the whole kidnapping. He bent low and slinked onward. There was nothing to hide behind, so if anyone spotted him, there wasn't much he could do about it.

He heard voices coming around the corner. He tried the closest door, discovered it was unlocked. He didn't know what was behind it, but he didn't have time to worry about that as he ducked into a big empty office with worn greige carpeting and off-white walls.

Chestnut whined softly until he put his finger to his lips.

He waited for the voices to pass, then waited for a few more moments before turning the knob.

It was locked.

Chestnut pressed against his legs and whined.

"What's wrong, girl?"

The far wall retracted into the floor, revealing a long row of giant saw blades.

Patty Perkins's voice emanated from a loudspeaker in the corner. "Hello, Mr. Bowen. Glad you could join us. We'll be running some tests."

The blades whirred to life, moving toward him.

"Please, try your best not to die," she said.

Chestnut cowered behind Byron's legs.

"This was your idea," said Byron.

She barked, flashing her puppy-dog eyes.

The blades moved slowly, giving him some time to think. He'd heard enough of Connie's stories to know that masterminds loved to play sadistic games. But they rarely created death traps without some kind of flaw, intentionally or not. If she were here, she'd see some small detail. Something innocuous like that generic painting of a sailboat regatta hanging beside the door.

Something like that.

He pulled the painting off the wall to reveal a small red button. He hesitated to push it. It couldn't be that easy.

The saws roared closer a few more inches.

He closed his eyes and jammed the button. The blades clicked off, receded back into their secret wall.

He leaned against the door. His heart thudded in his chest, though not as rapidly as it might once have. Dana was right.

He wasn't an adventurer, but one little diabolical death trap wasn't as big a deal as it would have been once.

"Not a difficult test," said Patty, "but admirably done."

He glared up at the speaker. "Why are you doing this?"

"I'll make you this promise," she said. "If you survive the next two tests, I'll tell you why."

The center of the carpet lit up.

"She doesn't think I'm a sucker, does she?" he asked Chestnut.

A bladed pendulum swung down from the ceiling, coming within a few inches of slicing off his nose. He hugged the wall as dozens more blades at various angles and heights swished in a deadly obstacle course.

"Oh, come on."

The wall vibrated as it pushed him unwillingly into the gauntlet.

"Oh, come on!"

Chestnut sprang, skipping between two pendulums, ducking beneath a third.

"No!" Byron reached for her, nearly losing his hand from a swinging scythe. He pressed himself against the wall, pushing back futilely. The flurry of blades came closer and closer, and he resolved not to scream, to face his gruesome demise with stoic strength so that when Connie saw this video later and avenged his death, she'd remember him as something other than shrieking in fear.

It was only when the blades all retreated back into the

ceiling that he realized he'd been screaming the whole time.
Also, crying a little.

Chestnut, wagging her tail, sat on the deactivation square.
Byron wiped away his tears and joined her.

"Hmm," said Patty. "I guess that counts. Now, one last test."

He braced himself for whatever was coming. A pylon rose
out of the floor. It opened to reveal two buttons.

"One of these buttons opens a door leading out of the
room. One triggers an explosive device under your feet. You
have exactly twenty seconds to push one or the bomb goes
off automatically."

"Do I get a hint?"

"This isn't a game show. Seventeen seconds."

"I know what you're doing. You're endangering me to see
if Connie will show up and save me."

She didn't reply.

"Well, I'm not going to push it," he said.

"Your call. Fifteen seconds."

He studied the buttons. There was nothing distinctive
about them. He walked around the pylon once to see if there
was something written on it. There wasn't.

"This is just random."

"Is it?" she replied. "Nine seconds."

"I don't suppose you have the answer," he asked Chestnut.
She barked.

"Six seconds," said Patty.

"Screw it." Byron pushed the button on the left.

He didn't explode.

A hidden door slid open. He approached with caution and stepped into a small, sparsely decorated room. It had a table and three chairs. A plate of gingersnaps sat on the table. Patty Perkins sat in one of the chairs. She was by herself. He seized the opportunity, fueled by adrenaline, and rushed at her. He knew it was a mistake even as he did it, but he had to take the chance.

He collided with a clear barrier splitting the room in half. Not hard enough to do any real damage, but hard enough to hurt.

She smiled from the other side of the barrier. "You probably have a lot of questions."

He rubbed his nose. "And you're going to answer them?"

"I'm not the bad guy."

"Most bad guys don't think they're bad guys."

Chestnut jumped onto one of the chairs. She stared at the gingersnaps.

"Yeah, go ahead if you want," said Byron.

She gulped down a couple of cookies.

"You must tell me where you got this dog," said Patty.

"Circus of crime," he replied, taking his own seat. "Larcenous animal trainer." He poured himself a glass of water. "So if you're not the bad guy, what's with the sadistic torture?"

She took a sip of her tea. "Do you remember when we first met that you asked me what kind of consultant I was?"

"Death-trap engineering?" he said.

"Too specific. I'm more of a general contractor. I help exceptional people of singular morality achieve their visions."

"You're a supervillain consultant?"

"Most of my clients prefer not to use the word 'villain,' but since it's just the three of us in this room, I'll own to that."

"So you're like a second-in-command?"

"I'm an independent operator. I don't have any interest in world domination or international extortion. But when someone does find themselves determined to conquer the world or maybe build an international criminal organization, they call me. I'm more than happy to help any wealthy idiot achieve their ambition."

"Which means what? You give them a pep talk and outfit them with death rays?"

"Sometimes. Depends on the client. Some come to me with a clear vision. Others have more general aspirations. I'm a middle woman. I know all the right people to help my clients achieve their goals, from branding and logos to building secret nuclear arsenals and moon bases."

"And torture rooms," added Byron.

"Now you're getting it."

"Basically, you're not a bad guy. You just enable bad guys."

"And get paid very well to do it."

"And now you want revenge on Connie for messing with your business."

She laughed.

"A megalomaniac spends millions building a criminal empire only to have someone like Connie waltz in and bring the whole thing crashing down. If that megalomaniac survives, they often come back to me with renewed ambitions. If they perish, there's always someone else eager to fill the void. Connie and her heroics are great for my bottom line. I'm the very best in my field, but it's a specialty that wouldn't be much use if any of my clients actually succeeded. Heck, I sometimes feel guilty that I've never given her a bonus for all her work on my behalf."

"And they come back to you, even after they fail?"

"It's never my fault they fail," she said. "I give them the tools. It's hardly my fault they can't use them properly."

"Still seems like a dangerous thing, working for supervillains."

"I've had to soothe more than a few egos in my day. Fortunately, I minored in child psychology. Comes in incredibly useful in this job."

"How come you've never run into Connie before?"

"My work is all done by the time she enters into it," said Patty. "Also, I'm not an idiot. I know not to tempt fate."

"None of this explains why you kidnapped me."

"I was just getting to that. It has nothing to do with Connie. Well, it is related. This is all about the caretaker mantle you inherited from her. Specifically, which part of it you ended up with. I assume Connie's mentioned her destined glorious death."

"Yes."

"I'm afraid it isn't her glorious death anymore. It's yours."

CONSTANCE VERITY DESTROYS THE UNIVERSE 183

"Connie doesn't believe in destiny."

"I wouldn't imagine she would. It's a loaded word anyway. Makes everything seem inevitable. Instead of thinking of it as a guiding force, imagine it as a suggestive one. Now that the Key is loose in the universe, you are meant to die in a very specific way."

"Then why are you trying to kill me?"

"Three reasons. The first is that a lot of this is conjecture. Hence the tests. Secondly, the small shard of caretaker you have within you isn't the whole thing. Connie has influenced the caretaker mantle as much as it has influenced her. Her every adventure, every brush with death, every last-minute escape reinforced her metaphysical role in the universe, making the caretaker stronger in the process.

"You, on the other hand, have mostly lived a boring life. The cosmos takes no special notice of you. If it wasn't for an accident, you'd never carry even the small caretaker piece you have. You might have a destiny. You might not. But if you do, it's a tiny sliver of one, more of a cosmic suggestion than an inevitable path."

"So it's like destiny, but not."

"Like I said, don't get hung up on the word. By placing you in peril and giving you the opportunity to survive, I'm hoping to nurture the sliver of caretaker within you, enabling it to rise to the occasion when most needed. Because you, Byron, need to die to save the universe."

Byron chuckled. "That's crazy."

"I've had a hard time convincing myself," she replied. "But that's just the way it is."

"And how do you know any of this?"

"You can't help but learn things in my line of work. And when I realized that the universe was going to end unless I stepped in, I stepped in. That's why I'm not the bad guy here, Byron. I'm just trying to help you save the universe."

"Out of the goodness of your heart?"

"There's no benefit to me if the universe is destroyed."

"You said there were three reasons you were trying to kill me. You only mentioned two."

Patty said, "We've had that death-trap model room for ages and never had the chance to use it before now."

She stood. Vents near the floor started pumping a neon-green gas in Byron's half of the room.

"Enjoyed the chat, but back to work. You have to face a lot more death before you're ready."

He could smell the faint rotten odor of the gas. Both the color and the odor had been added for his benefit.

"What if I refuse to play your game?" he asked.

"Then you'll die a very hideous death."

"But you said I'm destined—"

She shrugged. "Not destined. Suggested. And I've been wrong before."

Chestnut ate another gingersnap before jumping off her chair and running toward the exit. She paused, unwilling to go without him.

"Ah, damn it." He ran after her and out of the room, back into the death trap.

A grid of lasers crossed the room, flashing on and off in seemingly random patterns.

"Just touch the wall on the other side," said Patty over the speaker.

Chestnut took a step, but Byron stopped her.

"You stay here."

Then he closed his eyes and, screaming, ran toward his certain doom.

20

onnie had a problem with Nebraska. And that problem was that it was too close to Kansas.

Kansas, where dark gods waited to rise from their forgotten tombs and bring about the extinction of mankind.

Kansas, where all time travel led to a black void where a pale, wizened figure would greet you, playing a banjo and singing endless choruses of "Achy Breaky Heart."

Kansas, where Connie had come the closest to death on more than one occasion.

Kansas, her kryptonite.

In general, she did her best to steer clear of Nebraska, Colorado, Oklahoma, and Missouri. It wasn't always possible, and her experiences in those states were normal. She'd almost died in all of them, just as she'd almost died everywhere, when she thought about it. But she'd long ago accepted that there was something about Kansas to be avoided.

If she hadn't been on edge, she might not have even cared they were in Nebraska, but she resolved to get this done quickly and get out of here, which was standard operating procedure when Kansas was even tangentially involved.

Malady's entropy tracker led Connie, Tia, and Hiro to a castle outside Kearney, Nebraska. Connie studied it from the highway with a pair of binoculars.

"Looks like a modified shell keep design," said Connie.

"If I were an evil genius looking to lie low," said Tia, taking the binoculars, "maybe I'd think twice about building a castle in the Midwest."

"Masterminds," said Connie. "Most can't help themselves."

Tia handed Hiro the binoculars, but he waved them off.

"Don't you want to case the joint?" she asked.

Hiro chuckled. "I love it when you talk heist."

She smiled. "I know you do."

Hands in his pockets, he started walking toward the castle.

"You're doing it now?" she asked. "It's the middle of the afternoon. Don't you want cover of night?"

"What am I, an amateur?" he called back.

She pulled his suitcase from the trunk. "But you don't have your gear."

She glanced up, but he was gone, disappeared somewhere in the grassy field.

"That man," she said.

"You married him," said Connie.

"And I'm very glad she did," he said from behind Tia.

She didn't jump. She had a lot of practice at not jumping at his sudden appearances. And she had been half expecting it. It was something he loved to do.

"Hiro, this is important," said Connie. "I need you to take this seriously."

He saluted. "I always take my craft seriously." He opened the suitcase and grabbed a small tote bag full of smoke bombs and knockout darts and whatever other equipment he might need in a pinch. It wasn't much, but he'd explained that any ninja worth anything didn't require gear to do their job. Gear just made things easier.

"Like a shadow." He scooped Tia up in his arms, and they shared a long kiss. "Twenty minutes."

"Newlyweds," mumbled Connie.

Then he was gone, leaving Tia leaning against the car. Her lips were still puckered.

"You know he's just being how he is," said Tia. "He loves Byron."

Connie said, "Does he?"

"He likes Byron," said Tia. "More importantly, he knows how much you and I care for Byron. And maybe more importantly than that, his ego won't let him fail."

"That's your husband you're talking about."

"We love people for their faults. He is the best in the world at this."

On that, Connie had to agree.

—

Ajaw Cassowary was a man of singular destiny. He'd trained his mind and body to perfection. He'd carved a business empire that made him wealthy beyond measure, and when that bored him, he'd dabbled in true power. For Cassowary knew that he was not just to be a man of greatness. He was to be nothing less than a god.

His technicians lowered the Key into the transference device. Clamps locked the Key directly over a seat. The small orb of polished crystal could be held in one hand. But contained within it were unfathomable dangers and limitless power.

And that power would soon be his.

He instructed a technician to begin the transference process.

"But we haven't tested it, sir." The tech's voice cracked.

Cassowary grabbed the tech by his lab coat. "I will not be stifled by your cowardice."

"But, sir."

Cassowary broke the technician's neck and dropped the corpse like so much refuse. He grabbed another tech. "Now then, shall we begin the process?"

"Yes, sir." The tech saluted.

Cassowary took his seat beneath the Key as the laser drills moved into place and powered up. They would open the Key, and all its secrets would flow into him. Lesser minds might fear what was to come, but he could only smile.

The lasers fired. The ancient artifact trembled as hairline cracks ran along its surface. The light was blinding, but

Cassowary willed himself to look at it. He would bear witness to his ascension.

He noticed Hiro hanging from the scaffolding, reaching toward the Key.

And then the shell crumbled away, and untold cosmic power blinded him.

Connie was beginning to have doubts.

"It'll be fine," said Tia. "He's a super ninja. There's no way he got caught."

"Yeah. No way."

But Connie knew Hiro, knew his skills. If he'd said twenty minutes, he'd actually meant fifteen. And he wasn't back yet.

The sun was low in the sky, but it was still a few hours before dusk. Connie went to her suitcase and found her own gear.

"It's fine," said Tia.

"I'm just going to check on him," said Connie.

"And leave me here to worry about both of you?"

"I've got to do something."

"What are you going to do? Hiro is the best."

"I'm pretty good at infiltration myself," said Connie.

Tia put her hand on Connie's. "You are, but if security is good enough to catch him, you aren't getting through."

Connie studied the black hood in her hands. Tia was right about that.

"I'm sure it's fine," said Tia. "Just give him another five minutes."

Connie nodded. "Sure."

Thunder rumbled as the earth trembled. The wind picked up, howling, as the sky darkened to a deep red shade. Dozens of fissures cracked the grounds around the castle.

"Okay, so maybe everything isn't fine," said Tia.

The castle exploded. Not the whole thing, but a noteworthy portion of it. Chunks of brick rained down. Connie pulled Tia away as a wall's worth of rubble crushed their rental car.

Connie took a moment to clear her head. Considering the number of catastrophic explosions she encountered in an average week, it was a minor miracle that she'd managed to avoid tinnitus up to now.

The countryside fell deathly still, though the red skies remained. The half-ruined remnants of the castle collapsed quietly, almost apologetically.

Connie and Tia made their way to the rubble.

"I'm sure Hiro is okay," said Connie.

"Of course he is," said Tia. "He's always okay."

A few guards stumbled away from the castle. They were all too disoriented to try stopping Connie and Tia. The tracker in Connie's pocket beeped louder and faster with each step.

As they drew closer, it was clear the explosion hadn't followed the laws of physics. The rubble was brittle, breaking off in their fingers as they climbed over it. They walked past corpses, bleached skeletons still wearing their clothes.

"He's always okay," said Tia.

"Yeah."

Connie kept an eye out for any skeletons wearing Hiro's clothes. If there was even that left. There might be nothing. Not even a pile of bones.

The tracker beeped louder as they reached the epicenter. The air was thinner. Connie had no problem, but Tia had trouble breathing. She pushed on.

Connie picked up a massive piece of wall. It was easy. Too easy, in fact, as the wall floated into the air and hung there, ignoring gravity. They cleared away the rest of the debris without breaking a sweat.

Hiro lay curled up. Tia ran to his side and rolled him over.

"Goddamn it," she said. "If you're dead, I'm going to be so pissed at you."

The cloudless sky rumbled as lightning flashed across it.

Hiro sat bolt upright, causing Tia to jump. He drew in a painful breath.

"I'm not dead," he rasped, sounding as surprised as anyone there.

The ground quaked.

The tracker beeped louder as Connie took it out of her pocket.

"Tia, you might want to give Hiro some space."

A pile of rubble shifted as a figure pushed his way to his feet. A tall, broad man in a tattered suit lurched forward. Half the flesh had been burned off his face, but Connie still recognized him.

"Ajaw?"

Ajaw Cassowary stared daggers. "Verity! Of course it would be you. Who else would it be?"

"You can't blame me for this," she said. "I wasn't even here."

He laughed. Or tried to laugh. He stumbled, somehow still standing even through his injuries. "But you sent this fool to disrupt a very delicate experiment."

"I will not be held responsible for your faulty mad science," said Connie.

He took a clumsy step forward, adjusted the stub of a smoldering black tie. "You will not rob me of my destiny."

The ground quaked once more, harder. A swirling vortex overhead yanked random loose objects into the air and swallowed them.

"I feel weird," said Hiro.

A light appeared in his chest and burned a hole in his shirt.

The entropy tracker squealed.

"Tia, you need to get back from Hiro," said Connie.

"What's happening?" said Tia.

"Hiro, I think you absorbed the Key," said Connie, holding up the detector.

"How did that happen?" asked Tia.

Ajaw scratched at his face, peeling away pieces of loose skin that scattered in the wind like dust. "You're unworthy of this. You will give it to me."

"You were trying to bond with the Key?" said Connie.

"The Key is power," Ajaw said. "It will be mine. It will destroy this fool. And then the world. And then the universe. Give it to me. I alone have the singular strength of will to contain and control it."

"I don't know," said Hiro. "I don't feel bad. A little itchy."

He gulped. The beam of light in his chest flashed, disintegrating some rubble. He turned his back to them, covered the light with his hands. "That's going to be a problem."

"We'll get it out of you," said Connie.

Ajaw sprang with sudden energy, diving at Hiro. Connie tried to stop him by grabbing his arm, but the limb snapped off like a rotted branch.

With his remaining arm he seized Hiro by the shoulder. "Give it to me!"

A kaleidoscope of unearthly colors consumed Hiro. It washed over the area, and the world went quiet.

The lights ended as suddenly as they had begun.

Hiro stood beside the charred remnants of Ajaw Cassowary. The body fell over, crumbling into nothingness, but a disembodied scream of frustrated rage echoed for a few moments.

The light in Hiro's chest faded as he swallowed. They stood in a barren field. The castle, the rubble, every blade of grass, everything had been scoured clean away in a twenty-foot radius of him. All that remained was the black, cracked earth and Hiro, Tia, and Connie. And the ground under their feet felt mushy, like it'd dissolve if they stepped on it too hard.

"I can hold it." His breathing grew ragged. "I think."

Tia tromped across the squishy earth toward him.

"I don't think that's a good idea," said Connie.

Tia took his hand. Hiro stood with renewed strength.

"Hey, that is better. Thanks."

Connie checked the entropy tracker. The readings coming off Hiro were muted.

"It's like something is canceling out the Key," said Connie.

"Wave interference," said Tia. "The caretaker is the Key's opposite. I think I'm stabilizing it."

"I don't know if that's how wave interference works," said Connie. "And Bonita said that isn't right anyway."

"She also admitted she doesn't really know," said Tia, putting her arm around Hiro.

"Doctor Malady said if the Key and the caretaker came in contact, it'd unleash destructive force," said Connie.

"So he must have been wrong," said Tia. "Maybe it's because I'm carrying a smaller portion of it."

"That doesn't make sense."

"Does any of this?"

"I do feel better," said Hiro.

Connie couldn't argue with results, but she decided not to touch him. Just as a precaution.

"We'll take him back with us and get Perkins to extract the Key," she said.

"What if she can't?" asked Hiro.

"Well, then I guess I'll just have to stick tight with you for the long haul." Tia wrapped him in a hug and gave him a long kiss.

"Newlyweds," said Connie as they headed back to the highway.

21

Getting Hiro back to Patty proved more complicated than expected. As long as Tia stayed in contact, his body handled hosting the Key, and the chaos it created was minor. But their rental cars kept breaking down, and it was obviously folly to take a plane. When it became clear that they'd need a replacement car every hundred miles, they arranged for that ahead of time. They left a trail of broken axles and smoking engines across the interstate.

Along the way, Hiro began looking a little worse for wear. It started small, but he grew pale and clammy and started having coughing fits. Even with Tia and Connie to counteract the Key, its presence was taking a toll on his body.

"I look terrible," he said, checking himself in the mirror. He ran his fingers over his sallow cheeks and the bags under his eyes. "Oh God, why didn't it just kill me?"

Connie suppressed a grin. She didn't want anything serious to happen to Hiro, but he had betrayed her in the past. Multiple times. She was over it. She really was. But if he should be knocked down a peg or two before this was over, she allowed herself to enjoy it at least a little.

"Hush," said Tia. "I'll love you no matter how big that bald spot gets."

He felt the top of his head and groaned. "Not my hair! I love my hair! You love my hair!"

Hours later, their latest automobile casualty sputtered to a halt in front of Patty's building. All four tires spontaneously exploded.

They helped Hiro out. He was having trouble standing, leaning on them for support as he walked.

"Just a little while longer, honey," said Tia.

Connie had called ahead. As they entered the building, a cadre of technicians in lab coats appeared. They scrambled with clockwork precision, helping Hiro onto a gurney and taking readings of his vitals.

"Impressive," said Reynolds, his mustache twitching. "This man should be dead. The human body isn't capable of containing the Key."

"Focus, Reynolds," said Connie.

"Of course." They turned a corner as a tech handed him a tablet with the newest readings. "The fact that your friend here hasn't disintegrated by now testifies to his tremendous willpower."

"Ninja training." The last bit of color drained from Hiro. "Second to none."

"If you mean he's stubborn, then yes, I can attest to that," said Tia.

"Love you, too, honey," said Hiro.

"You can have the Key when you take it out of Hiro," said Connie. "I assume you can do that."

Reynolds said, "We can. I think."

"Think or know?" asked Connie.

"I hesitate to make promises."

She grabbed him by the collar. "Make promises."

He nodded enthusiastically. "We can."

Tia wiped some sweat from Hiro's face. "Sooner rather than later would be preferable."

They entered a lab. More technicians were busy at work, and Hiro, Tia holding his hand, was wheeled to the center of the room, where a big red circle had been stenciled on the floor. Workers moved emitter dishes and connected conduits.

Byron and Chestnut stood to one side in the only area that was bustle-free.

Connie hugged him. "Are you okay?"

"I'm fine. What's wrong with Hiro?"

"It'll work itself out," said Connie. "Are you sure you're okay? You seem off."

She turned his head to the side to check for any signs of a mind-control implant. Or plastic surgery scars. Or anything else suspicious.

"I'm fine," he said.

He didn't sound fine.

"I'm just distracted, and I can't wait to go home."

The answer was plausible enough that she decided not to pick at it for the moment.

"We're going to need some space for the process," said Reynolds to Tia. "I'm afraid you'll have to step aside."

"But if I let go—"

"He should be fine for the few minutes necessary. If you're touching him, it will interfere with the extraction field matrix."

"Science stuff. Got it." She leaned close and kissed Hiro. "Just hold it together a little while longer. I know you can."

"Holding it together is one of the ninjaly virtues," he wheezed with a pained smile. "Relax. I can handle it."

Tia let go of his hand and stepped reluctantly away to join Connie and Byron.

"Do we trust these people?" Tia whispered.

Connie said, "No, but we have to see this play out. I swear to you if anything happens to Hiro . . ." She took Tia's hand and gave it a squeeze. "I won't let anything happen to Hiro."

Connie assessed the situation. Five guards were scattered among the tech personnel on the floor level. Three more wandering the catwalks, looking down on them.

The doctors attending to Hiro stepped back as a warning claxon sounded. Reynolds stood at the control panel and adjusted a few dials. "Everything looks good. Beginning containment sequence."

He flipped a plastic cover off a big red button and pushed it without ceremony.

The lab machinery hummed to life, filling the air with a low static that caused everyone's hair to frizz. Hiro went limp as a shimmering blot of something crawled out of his chest. It slithered around silently.

Connie had seen creatures from outside time and space before. Plenty of times. But they always ended up taking some form while in the universe. Every time this thing almost solidified into something tangible and knowable, it quickly returned to a shapeless mass. This was a form, of sorts, but the barest minimum of one. And as it rolled and sloshed around, it burned holes in the air, in the fabric of reality itself.

Reynolds turned a dial. The lab's lights dimmed as more power was channeled into the machinery. The thing floated out of Hiro, still connected by a thin strand of itself.

"We have containment!" said Reynolds.

"And extraction?" asked Patty.

"Not possible," he replied.

"Shame," she said.

Another claxon sounded. Blast shields lowered over Hiro and the Key. Guards came streaming into the lab. They surrounded Connie, Tia, and Byron.

"Same side," said Connie derisively.

"It's complicated," said Patty. "I'm not any happier about it than you are. But we can't save Hiro."

"But you said you could," said Tia.

"An optimistic lie. If we could do it, we would. But this

is the universe we're talking about. One life isn't too big a sacrifice to make."

"That's easy to say when it's not your life," said Byron.

Patty said, "Look. This is not what I expected. I thought when I sent Connie to collect the Key that it would bond with her. And then she would safely bring it here and I would contain her and the Key, destroying her as part of her glorious death. But we both know that's not how it worked out, don't we, Byron?"

"What's she talking about?" asked Connie.

"It's nothing," he said.

"Beginning containment protocol," said Reynolds, punching a bigger, redder button. The machinery screeched as the emitters bombarded Hiro with untested, impossible scientific engineering.

Hiro tensed, and the Key fluctuated wildly, changing colors and shape. There was a hypnotic quality to it. The human mind wasn't made to see it, and that unknowable nature made some retch and drew others toward it. A technician fell to her knees and vomited. Another ran screaming from the room, clawing at his own eyes. Several others stood transfixed.

Patty had her back to it, and Reynolds was too engrossed in running the machinery to care. Connie and Tia and Byron were unaffected. Wave interference from the caretaker, possibly. Or simply that they'd seen plenty of weird stuff over the years, and this was not appreciably weirder.

Chestnut, perhaps by virtue of being a dog, didn't seem to care about the Key.

Connie sidled toward the nearest guard, who was half watching her and half watching the Key. She only needed a distraction. She slipped the Strand of Hemsut from her wrist and hoped the universe hadn't stopped wanting her dead.

"You can't save everybody," said Patty.

"I can try," said Connie.

"But even you know that there's always a price. How many times have you paid it? How many times have you done what needed to be done for the greater good?"

"Are you giving me the 'We're not so different' speech? Or the 'Necessary sacrifice' speech? Because either way, I've heard them both before. And I can tell you that they're bull-shit. We are different. Very different. And people who talk about life as a balance are always talking about doing some-thing wrong and using some half-assed preserve-the-balance rationalization afterward."

Patty looked as if she might argue, but she stopped herself. "Okay. Maybe I'm the bad guy. But when the universe survives into the next hour, I think I can live with myself. And if it's any consolation, Hiro was dead the moment the Key bonded with him instead of you. Nothing could've changed that."

Tia punched Patty square in the face. "Screw you."

A new alarm sounded, though it was hard to hear it over the warning sirens going off already. The sound of several explosions popped in the distance.

Patty wiped her bloody nose. "What did you do, Constance?"

Connie held up the strand. "Just being me."

"We're under attack," shouted a minion. "Multiple breaches." He handed Patty a tablet showing security footage.

She shoved it back into his chest. "Doesn't matter. It's too late to stop."

The Key shrank into a small collection of glittering madness. Hiro lay very still.

"We will save the universe, despite your misguided heroics. Initiate obliteration protocol, Reynolds." Patty paused with a sudden realization. "Huh. That does sound a lot like mastermind talk, doesn't it?"

"If it walks like a duck . . . ," said Connie.

"In for a penny, I suppose," said Patty as her guards closed in on Connie, Tia, and Byron. "Wait. What happened to the dog?"

The machinery stopped. Its overwhelming static hum shut off, replaced by confused murmuring from the technicians.

Chestnut, tail wagging, came from behind an access panel. She dropped several fuses at Connie's feet.

Patty frowned. "That is a very well trained dog."

A team of commandoes burst into the lab, engaging Patty's forces in a firefight.

A blocky walking tank crashed through a wall. It leveled its cannons at Connie.

"And now, Snurkab, it is with great regret that I must destroy you."

"Hello, Blog," said Connie.

The Key expanded and pulsed. It growled, and the blast shields melted.

"Containment failing!" said Reynolds.

To punctuate the observation, part of the machinery exploded, sending technicians and commandoes above plummeting from the catwalks. A sizeable chunk of the containment device was violently ejected and landed on Blog's tank, burying it under tons of smoldering weird scientific debris.

The Key settled back into Hiro, who sat up and surveyed the lab.

Tia stepped forward. "Hiro?"

He looked at her, through her. As if the mere idea of her confused him. He stepped off the gurney.

"He's gone," said Patty. "And you've killed the universe."

Security guards surrounded Hiro. They unloaded rounds of automatic fire into him, but the bullets evaporated in midair. He smiled slightly as a wave of energy pulsed from him, disintegrating the guards in a flash, knocking everyone else in the lab down. Everyone but Connie, Tia, and Byron.

Tia touched Hiro, and they both glowed. Streams of energy coursed from their bodies to Connie and Byron.

"Wave interference," said Connie.

She grabbed Hiro's arm. The light intensified, and the lab trembled.

Patty shouted to Byron. "You have to stop it!"

"How?"

"I don't know! It's not my destiny!"

Byron took a step forward. Hiro's head snapped toward him. Byron reached out toward Hiro, and the tendrils of energy connected with Hiro, Connie, Tia, and Byron. Connie, Tia, and Byron fell to their knees as their bodies burned with alternating waves of heat and cold.

"What's happening, Reynolds?" asked Patty.

"I don't know. Why would I know?"

Hiro started laughing.

Connie managed to rise to her feet. Screaming, she tackled Hiro, knocking him to the floor. The energy matrix dissolved as she held him down with a leg lock.

"What do we do?" asked Byron, struggling to catch his breath.

"I don't know," replied Tia, pushing herself to her own feet.

The aura around Connie and Hiro burned brighter. Everyone shielded their eyes except for Byron and Tia, who felt drawn to it, moving forward against their own will.

"No," said Connie. "Stay back!"

Yelling, she pulled all the power into her, struggling to tame and control it.

Bonita teleported onto the scene. She used her antennae to shade her eyes. "What the hell?"

Then Connie and Hiro exploded.

Tia was surprised she wasn't dead. Hanging out with Connie led to plenty of brushes with death. So much so that it was expected that if there was a way to survive, they'd find it. But the lab had exploded with such force that she didn't see how she could manage. However, the fact that she realized the lab had exploded told her that she was still alive.

Bonita adjusted the force-field generator on her belt. "Everybody alive?"

Tia studied the energy dome covering her, Byron, Chestnut, Patty, Reynolds, and Bonita. On the other side, the lab was in smoking ruins. The final standing bits of the containment machine teetered, then collapsed into wreckage.

Byron checked himself, then Chestnut. She licked his hands and wagged her tail.

"What the hell happened?" he asked.

"That's what I was wondering," said Bonita. Her wings fluttered in confusion, though no one else understood her body language enough to recognize that.

Blog's walking tank wrenched itself half-free from the wreckage that pinned it. He swept the room with his one barely working cannon. "Nice try, Snurkab, but . . . hey, where did she go?"

"They blew up," said Tia.

"No," said Patty. "It's much worse than that."

The lab's fire suppression systems burst into flame.

22

Special Agent Lucas Harrison had once known things. Important things. Secrets of the universe that few were fortunate or unfortunate enough to know. Although at times it seemed like more people knew than not and that everyone was in on the conspiracy. It was probably the company he kept then, because now he didn't know much of anything and lived his life accordingly. And nobody cared, least of all Harrison himself.

He still worked for the government, though it was no longer the secret government that ran the world, or at least always claimed to. It was the regular old government that did regular old government business. He sat at a desk for eight hours a day, filed paperwork and approved requisitions and stamped forms and kept his head down, and went home at the end of the day feeling quietly discontent with his lot in life. This wasn't much different from when he was in the know, so the transition was easy enough.

He unlocked the door to his apartment. The door snagged on something, prevented from opening more than halfway. He squeezed through, past the body crumpled between the door and the wall.

"Huh."

He set his sack of groceries down and checked the body. The person was unconscious. The gray suit, the shades, the ten-millimeter pistol cradled loosely in his hand. Hadn't even gotten a shot off.

"Huh."

This smacked of conspiracy business, but he wasn't important enough to kill. Not anymore. Probably never had been, though that wouldn't always prevent some people from pulling the trigger on a cleanup protocol. But it was a little late for that now.

It took him longer than it should have to process all this. He'd never been a good field agent. Years at a desk hadn't helped. He reached for his piece with a sigh, only to realize, with another sigh, that he didn't have one. He'd left it at work, where it usually stayed locked in his desk drawer.

"Come on, Lucas," he grumbled. "Get it together, man."

In a bit of a fugue, he went to his kitchenette and set down his sack of groceries. He returned to the living room, and only then did he think to turn on the lights and check for more intruders. He was still unarmed. Hadn't even thought to get a knife out of the kitchen.

Did he have any clean knives?

Connie sat on his couch. Her hands were folded over her crossed legs. There were another two goons in gray suits unconscious at her feet. A fourth was slung halfway over the coffee table.

"Huh."

She uncrossed her legs, folded her arms. "You're welcome."

"Uh, yeah. Thanks. Not that I'm complaining, Connie, but what are you doing here? Been a couple of years since I've seen you."

She glanced out the window, at the view of an alley. The stink of the dumpster outside could seep into the apartment on hot days like this.

"Saving your life, apparently," she said.

The agent on the coffee table tried to get up. She chopped him with one of her fancy kung fu strikes, and he fell limp.

She turned her attention to the front door. "I'll get it."

A moment later, someone knocked.

Harrison made a sweeping gesture. "Be my guest."

She answered the door. He heard a short scuffle, but he decided it wisest to stay out of the way and let her do her job. She returned, dragging a new unconscious guy.

"That's the last of them," she said. "They'll be out for a few hours."

"Why were they trying to kill me? I don't rate a hit squad."

"I don't know," she said. "I just know you're safe. You should call Agent Ellington. You can trust her."

"Jeez." He pulled his phone from his pocket. "I don't even know if I have her number."

Connie took the phone, typed Ellington into his contacts, handed it back. "That's the priority number. She'll answer."

"Thanks. I guess I owe you another one, Verity."

But by the time he looked up from his phone, she was gone.

Susan Lash, rogue archeologist, knocked out the last temple guardian with a solid right hook. He fell screaming into the foggy abyss below. Guido, her trusty pilot and sidekick, picked up her shoulder bag and handed it to her.

"Where do these guys always come from?" he asked.

They crossed the bridge over the chasm and approached the thirty-foot-tall idol to an ancient forgotten god. It sat cross-legged, cradling a burning crystal orb.

"Pre-Atlantean, I'd say," remarked Lash.

The orb burned brighter by the moment. She removed her hat and wiped the sweat from her forehead.

"It's going critical. I'd say we have about a minute before everything in a ten-mile radius is vaporized."

Shielding her eyes, Lash depressed an icon on the idol's base. A massive keyboard with hundreds of stone buttons slid out. She studied the symbols. "Fortunately, I've a working understanding of pre-Atlantean logograms, as well as a passing knowledge of artifacts of this nature."

She pushed an icon of a bird with its wings spread, followed by a symbolic representation of the solar system. The orb crackled.

"All part of the process," she said.

A shrieking warrior sprang from nowhere. He jammed Guido in the shoulder with a spear. Lash pulled her revolver and shot the guardian twice. She checked on Guido.

"I've had worse," he said. "Turn that thing off."

She pushed a few more buttons, and the orb hummed like a horde of angry bees. She paused. "I don't remember which one of these two depicts sunrise or sunset."

"Better pick one quick," said Guido, ripping a bandage from his own shirtsleeve to wrap around his wound.

The orb split as glowing liquid fire dripped from it.

Lash reached for an icon.

Connie caught her hand.

"It's the other one," she said. "The one with the nesting bird."

"Of course!" Lash pushed the ancient button.

The orb was extinguished instantly. The artifact shattered. All the pieces fell harmlessly into the idol's outstretched hands.

"Can't believe I almost made that mistake. I don't know why you're here, Verity, but I'm just glad you are."

But Constance was gone.

The creature had been born of twisted science and strange alchemy. It was only a few hours old, but those moments had been filled with terror. It woke up on a table, struggling to make sense of its nightmarish existence.

It ran through the darkened night, through the thickened woods, pursued by baying hounds. And behind those hounds, a mob with flashlights and pitchforks and bloodlust. There was no escape. The creature sensed this, but still it ran, driven by a primal need to survive.

It scrambled across fallen trees and rocks, sloshed its way across a muddy river. It clawed for every moment of life it might have before death reclaimed it once again. Its flight came to an end at a ravine, where its only choice was to wait for the mob to tear it to pieces or to jump into the darkness on the slim hope that it might survive the fall. Panting, rasping, it took the step.

"Hey, don't do that," said Connie, pulling it back by the arm.

The exhausted creature looked down at her. She was small, but everything was small compared to its massive frame. It turned away from her, covered its scarred face with its scarred hands.

"We can handle this," she said as she gently pulled its hands down. "Believe me, as monsters of twisted science go, you're actually pretty handsome."

She smiled, and the creature smiled back.

The mob burst forth. The huge creature stepped behind Connie. A man in a worn baseball cap and flannel vest pushed his way forward. He pointed his shotgun at Connie and the creature.

"Step aside, lady. We've got no quarrel with you. Just this godless abomination."

"That's not happening," said Connie.

"It killed a dog!" shouted a woman somewhere in the crowd.

"Did you kill anyone?" Connie asked the creature. "It's okay to be honest with me."

The creature shook its head.

"You're going to take that thing's word over ours?" asked the leader.

"Right now," said Connie, "he's not the one pointing a shotgun at me."

The leader nodded to a pudgy man beside him. "Get her out of the way."

Sneering, the pudgy goon reached for Connie. She kicked him in the groin, and he fell over.

"You can't fight us all," said the leader.

The creature pushed Connie aside and beat its chest as it bellowed. It picked up a huge rock and reared back to throw it into the crowd.

"No!" said Connie, jumping between the crowd and the creature's rage. "You don't have to do that!"

The creature hesitated.

"Kill it!" shouted someone, and the mob started chanting.

"For Christ's sake." Connie snatched the leader's shotgun and fired it once in the air.

Everything went quiet.

"Maybe," she said, "just maybe we don't have to kill each other right now. Can we give it a minute to sort things out? Is that too much to ask?"

The creature set down the rock. The crowd murmured. The hounds kept barking.

"I've been in this type of situation before," she said. "And

I can tell you right off that the monster is rarely the actual monster. And I'm sorry to call you a monster. I don't mean that."

The creature mumbled and shrugged.

"So did anyone actually see him kill this dog?" she asked.

"Bernice saw it," said a tall man in the crowd.

"No, I didn't see it," said Bernice somewhere in the back. "It was Chett."

"I didn't see it," said Chett. "Nicole is the one who told me about it."

"I heard it from Bob. It was his dog."

"None of my dogs are dead," said Bob.

The mob mumbled.

"Well, why didn't you say anything before?" asked the leader.

"I didn't know it was supposed to be one of my dogs. Nobody told me."

Connie cleared her throat and the crowd went quiet again. "Has anyone here actually had a dog killed tonight?"

The mob spent a full minute checking among themselves. Finally, the leader said, "Well, shit. That's embarrassing."

"Do you have something to say?" asked Connie.

"Yeah, uh, sorry about that."

"It's still a godless abomination!" shouted someone.

"Ah, Hilda, nobody asked you," replied someone else.

Connie handed the leader back his shotgun. "Now, are we going to play nice?"

"Yes. Sorry about that."

A grandmotherly woman approached the creature. "You look like you could use a nice meal."

The creature cautiously took her hand, and she led it through the crowd and back toward town.

"I guess we owe you thanks, Ms. . . . Say, we didn't catch your name."

But Connie was gone.

Jonathan Zhou lay strapped to the rack on wheels. Buchanan Buckingham laughed. It was too delicious having Zhou finally at his mercy.

"I've already alerted the world governments about your nefarious scheme," said Zhou. "Even if you kill me, you'll never get away with it."

Buckingham sipped his cognac. He smirked, raising an eyebrow. "My dear Agent Zhou, you've been a thorn in my side far too often. Foiled too many of my grand designs. But not this time."

He pushed a button on his chair. The sliding doors opened and a tall redhead in a sequined gown entered.

Zhou said, "Marlene. But you're—"

"Dead?" Buckingham laughed again. "I'm afraid the lovely Marlene Byrne has been working for me this whole time. Surprised?"

The evil genius stood. He was tall and lean, and he walked with the creeping gait of a stalking spider.

"You mustn't be too harsh on her. I do hold her father hostage. Such a foolish thing, familial bonds. A weakness to be exploited."

She looked away from Zhou. "I'm sorry, Jonathan."

He lowered his head and hung on the rack.

"Do you know how long I've waited for this moment?" said Buckingham. "Ah, to savor this victory. And to see you betrayed by your own love." He blew a kiss.

"What do you want?" asked Zhou.

"I have what I want. Now the only thing left to do is execute you before the very eyes of the woman you love."

"You're a sadistic madman."

"And you, Agent Zhou, are no longer my concern." He snapped his fingers, and a henchagent placed a small device in his hand. "With a push of this button, you shall be dropped into my mutant piranha tank. They'll strip the flesh from your bones within seconds. A quick death, at least, a small mercy I'll grant you."

His finger hovered over the button for a few glorious moments. With one last wry chuckle, he pushed it.

Nothing happened.

He stabbed at the button repeatedly.

"Well, this is vexing. Did you put fresh batteries in this thing?" he asked his minion.

She nodded. "Yes, sir."

He handed it to her and pushed the rack to one side. He stamped on the trapdoor. It didn't budge.

"Oh, I think I figured it out," said the minion. "I forgot to turn it on." She flicked the small switch on the side and pushed the button. The trapdoor opened. Buckingham, with one foot on it, almost fell in.

"Careful, you dolt!"

"My bad," said the minion. She pressed a second button on the remote, and the rack shackles released Jonathan Zhou. He jumped to his feet, then caught the nearest guard by surprise, knocking his opponent to the floor and taking his machine gun.

A pair of guards tried to shoot Zhou, but the incompetent minion sprang, defeating them with two swift Martian kung fu nerve strikes.

"Damn you, Zhou!" Buckingham pulled his gun. Before he could aim, Marlene grabbed a rusty fire poker from a tray of torture implements and bashed him over the head. He toppled into the open piranha tank. He screamed only once before the churning water turned crimson.

Zhou and Marlene embraced.

"Can you ever forgive me?" she asked.

They kissed, long and deep.

Connie pulled off her minion hood as she kicked a guard attempting to get back up. "Time for that later, lovebirds. You'll find your father in the biochemical lab, subfloor three, Marlene. The self-destruct for the doomsday device is in the control room next door."

"How did you get here, Connie?" asked Zhou.

"Long story," she said.

"However you did, the world owes you a great debt."

But Connie was gone.

"We really should change the logo," said Larry Peril, leafing through a portfolio of proposals. "And probably the name."

His bodyguard, Apollonia, piloted the supersonic jet. "I like the logo. And the name."

"It doesn't fit anymore," he said. "Siege Perilous. It's sinister."

"Not necessarily," she said.

"You're telling me that if a jet showed up with food and medicine and this logo"—he held up an illustration of a sword dangling over the world—"and that name, you'd trust them?"

"I don't trust anyone," she said. "But it's a fair point."

Larry sat back in the copilot seat and glanced through potential new logos. "It'd be a shame to lose the branding, but it doesn't scream 'trustworthy.'"

The plane shuddered as something crashed in the back.

"I thought everything was locked down back there," said Larry.

"It was." Apollonia set the autopilot and pulled her gun. "Stay here."

Crates of relief supplies crowded the hold. She moved through the aisles, scanning for trouble. She found a puddle of hydraulic fluid, the kind used in old Siege Perilous robot soldier prototypes.

Lady Peril had experimented with the idea but ultimately decided they were distasteful. The prototypes were disassembled, but every so often, one was discovered in a locked-away corner of a Siege Perilous base in a crate that might very easily be mistaken for just another container of food and medicine.

Sometimes, the robots might activate on their own. Larry was right. The logo had to go.

"Is everything all right?" shouted Larry.

"Get back in the cockpit! Lock the door!"

Hydraulic fluid dripped on her shoulder. She spun and fired, but the robot was already on her. It pinned her to the floor and snapped the mechanical jaws on its skull-like head.

Apollonia shoved with her legs, managing to push the robot off her. It clacked its jaws and studied her with its glowing red eyes.

"God, I've always hated these fucking things." She fired, blowing out one of its optical sensors.

"What's happening?" shouted Larry.

The robot scrambled over a crate, toward Larry's voice. Apollonia ran after it, but she heard Larry's scream and knew it would be too late.

She found him splattered with oil.

Connie stood over the twitching robot with the emergency fire axe in her hands. With two more swings, she decapitated the killer prototype, then buried the axe into its chest. She wiped some of the oil from her face.

"I'm not going to ask how you got here," said Larry. "I'm just glad you're here."

But she was gone.

23

The lab was in ruins, but the break room several floors above was mostly untouched. A piece of shrapnel had destroyed the refrigerator, and half of its floor was torn away, exposing dangling bits of infrastructure. The coffee maker had fallen into the resulting void, forcing Patty and Reynolds to explain the situation to Tia, Bonnie, and Byron over a cup of instant coffee.

"We were hoping to nip this in the bud," said Reynolds. "If you hadn't interfered, there was every indication the Key could have been contained again."

"We weren't going to just let you kill my husband," said Tia.

He said, "You didn't save him, and now you've unleashed the end of the universe."

"We knew it was a long shot," said Patty. "No need to point fingers."

"Years of research, millions of dollars, down the drain," said Reynolds.

Patty said, "We can worry about that later. We need to focus on the task at hand."

"She's right," said Tia. "Whenever things get crazy, always concentrate on what you can do. Not on what you can't. But I do have a question. Why are you here, Bonita?"

"I'd finished running the simulations," said Bonita. She'd taken on her human form, since it made interacting with these primitive creatures easier. "I would've been here sooner, but I couldn't track Connie herself. Something was obscuring her."

"The Strand of Hemsut," said Tia.

"If I'd been here sooner, I might have been able to stop what happened. You humans should never have interfered in things you couldn't possibly understand."

She projected a 4D holographic equation. Just looking at it gave Tia a headache.

Reynolds said, "Hey, I think you missed a zero there."

Bonita smirked. "I won't be taking math advice from a species that still believes in the existence of the graviton." She zoomed in on the equation and frowned. "Well, damn it."

She started making corrections.

"If Connie and Hiro aren't dead, where are they?" asked Byron.

"Everywhere. Nowhere," said Patty. "Wherever they need to be."

"What the hell does that mean?"

"It's complicated," said Reynolds. He squinted at Bonita's

equation. "It doesn't look like you've taken into account the quantum flux variant."

Bonita grunted, glaring at the human. But she and Reynolds went to the corner of the break room and conferred.

Patty said, "I can't claim to understand it very well. Reynolds might be the most brilliant mind on Earth, and even his grasp is unreliable at best. And your alien friend seems to have made her own mistakes. But I can tell you what we do know.

"The caretaker and the Key are connected. When the Key was found and liberated, the caretaker responded. Like an echo, a balancing force. As the threat posed by the Key has now grown exponentially, so has Connie's role as caretaker."

"That's good, right?" asked Byron. "If anyone can beat this thing, it has to be Connie."

"This isn't a villain or a mastermind or even an all-powerful god-computer we're talking about," said Patty. "It's a concept, a primal force. How does one person, even someone like Constance Verity, defeat the idea of inevitable entropy? It's our belief that the caretaker within her functions as a sort of metaphysical antibody. At full power, it would destroy the Key. Or at least, send it back to where it came from."

"That's an oversimplification," interrupted Reynolds. "And the antibody analogy is way off."

Tia's cell rang. She answered. "Hey, Harrison, I'm a little busy here." She stood. "What? No, Connie's not with us. Wait. Have you seen her?"

She walked into the corner to carry on the conversation.

"Details," said Patty. "The point is that through unforeseen circumstances, the caretaker is currently split among three hosts. Connie has most of it, but not all of it." She set her cup down and looked directly at Byron. "And maybe not the most important part."

"You're saying I'm the anti-Key?" asked Byron.

Patty said, "We have good reason to believe it."

"Then why did Connie tell me to stay back?"

"Clearly, she's motivated by her vaunted sense of heroism. She's unwilling to let you die."

Tia ended her call. "Weird. That was Lucas Harrison. Connie just saved his life a while ago."

"Great. So we know where to find her now," said Byron.

"She isn't there anymore. He says she just . . . disappeared."

Her cell rang again. "Hi, Larry. We're in the middle of—she what?" Tia left the room to continue the call.

"I know it's not something you want to hear," said Patty to Byron. "But you'll have to do what Connie doesn't have the strength to do."

"Or maybe Connie has better instincts than you give her credit for," said Byron.

Bonita closed the projection. "It's no use. The Key's influence is spreading. It's impossible to predict what might actually happen."

"Okay, so let's assume that Connie and Hiro are still out there," said Byron. "How are we supposed to find them?"

Tia came running into the room. "I know what we have to do! If we can't go to Connie, we get her to come to us."

"And how do we do that?" asked Patty.

"We destroy the world."

24

onnie knew what she had to do.

She materialized in the street. She yanked the man out of the way of a speeding car.

"Thank you," he said.

"You're welcome," she said absently. He was no longer important enough to warrant her attention.

She entered a nearby convenience store, bought a case of bottled water and several sandwiches. No sooner had she paid for them than she felt the pull of the universe, taking her where she needed to be.

From the outside, the teleportation might seem instantaneous, but from her perspective, it took a few moments. Not any exact amount of time, since she traveled through an infinite void where time and space followed different rules. The whole place had a light blue tint to it, but it had no up or down. It was nowhere and everywhere at once, and just glimpsing it would have driven most people into catatonia. But she'd seen weirder things.

She floated in the emptiness, clutching her bag of convenience-store rations. It was quiet here, and she could close her eyes and clear her head from the jumble of thoughts racing through it. Not all those thoughts were her own. They were cosmic directions, given to her by the caretaker. The foreign instructions whispered to her as they had her whole life. She'd just never realized it before.

But she knew what she had to do.

She dropped into time and space. Gravity and air pressure exerted themselves, and she landed in the middle of an overgrown forest. She made her way to a hiker with her legs pinned under a fallen tree.

"It's okay," said Connie.

The hiker glanced up at Connie's sudden appearance. "Oh, thank God. I didn't think anyone would find me in time."

Connie held up the bottled water and sandwiches. "This will be enough to keep you alive until help gets here."

"Wait? You're not going to get this tree off me?"

"No time," said Connie. "You'll be fine. It's just another day and a half."

The hiker said, "But you can't just leave me—"

"There's no time," said Connie. "If I don't go now, the prime minister of a thousand-world empire dies. The resulting war will cost billions of lives."

"Oh." The hiker looked at Connie with a strange mix of gratitude and fear.

"You don't understand," said Connie.

She thought about explaining with the minute or two she had to spare here, but it would only confuse the hiker. It was enough that she would survive now. In fifteen years, she'd invent a cure for some disease. Connie didn't know which one exactly—she didn't need to know—but it was one of the big ones.

Connie set the supplies beside the hiker. She rifled through the hiker's pack. "I need your axe and flashlight."

"But I need those—"

"No, you don't. You'll be fine. Thirty-two hours."

Connie closed her eyes, listening to the whisper as the cosmic consciousness updated itself. The universe was a big, complicated thing. Every action rippled throughout. Adjustments had to be made.

"Thirty-three hours."

The forest fell away as she was plucked into the space between spaces again. She heard the countless things going wrong at this moment. The universe was broken. She saw that now. But she would fix it. She had the power. She finally knew what she had to do.

She materialized on an alien world in a council chamber. Her senses snapped into focus, and she pulled the prime minister out of his chair as one of his traitorous advisers blasted a hole in it with a laser pistol concealed in his long-sleeved robe.

She threw the axe, striking the adviser in the shoulder. She bounded over the minister's desk, punched the adviser in his fishlike face. He fell, dropping his pistol. She caught it before it hit the ground, twirled around, and shot the gun out of another adviser's tentacles.

The guards burst into the chamber.

"Destroy her!" said the fish adviser.

"Wait." The prime minister pulled himself to his feet. "This is the Legendary Snurkab, and I believe she has just saved my life."

A third adviser drew a dagger from his robe and, with a warbling screech, took a step toward the minister.

Connie clobbered the would-be-assassin with the handle of her flashlight.

In a few minutes, the traitorous politicians were being led away. The prime minister bowed to her.

"It appears that the universe owes you great thanks again—"

He went on, but she wasn't listening. Not to him.

"You're welcome," she said, interrupting whatever speech he was in the middle of. "If you want to thank me, you'll give me your long coat."

"My coat? But this very coat is symbolic of my office, worn by a dozen of my predecessors. I can have a copy made if—"

She snapped her fingers. She had no patience for this. She didn't need to explain herself.

"Of course," he said. "Anything for you, honorable Snurkab."

He slipped off the garment. She tossed it across her shoulder. "Thanks."

The chamber disappeared.

She materialized near the summit of Gangkhar Puensum in the middle of a heavy snow. She put on the long coat. It automatically adjusted to her dimensions and heated up to compensate for the low temp. The pockets dinged politely as they manufactured a pair of gloves for her. She slipped them on and trudged a bit farther up the mountain. The snow made it hard to see, but she didn't need to. She knew where she was going.

She found the cave where she knew it to be and used the flashlight to light her way as she plunged deeper. She came across the huge cosmic egg in the back. With some effort, she rolled it out into the open air, and she gave it several good whacks with her flashlight handle. It cracked open, and the great golden hamsa bird sprang forth, fully formed. It spread its rainbow-colored wings.

Connie covered her eyes. "Don't suppose I could trouble you for a feather?"

The hamsa flapped its wings, launching itself into the sky. The snowstorm died down. The bird had been hidden ages ago from a god long dead, but its return would herald the birth of an enlightened soul who would bring about a new era of peace and prosperity. She had no time to think about that right now.

She grabbed the single radiant feather left in the shell. It would be just the thing she needed to restore the dying forest spirit of Sundarbans. But first, she'd have to foil a

kidnapping in Chicago. She pocketed the feather and checked
her laser gun.

The universe whispered, and she listened.

She knew what she had to do.

Connie disappeared.

25

onnie stood in a small room at the end of time. It wasn't much to look at, but at least it was quiet. The needy whispers of the universe were gone. There were no disasters to be averted, no more lives to save. There was only the vast, empty silence.

"Thank God."

The room overlooking the dying gasps of the last star was sparsely furnished. But it had a chair, which she promptly collapsed into.

The door opened, and a short reptilian creature entered, pushing a cart before it.

"Welcome," she said. "We've been waiting for you."

Connie sat up. "For me? Or someone like me?"

"Is there a difference?" The reptile rolled the dessert cart before Connie. "You're probably hungry. Please, help yourself."

Connie poured herself some water and bit into a chocolate donut with sprinkles.

Her host smiled, smoothed her robes. "I have a database of all known species that have ever existed in the universe and a very efficient kitchen."

Connie said, "So what's the deal? Are you one of those last surviving members of an ancient progenitor civilization?"

The reptile coiled her long tail beneath her and used it as a seat. "How'd you figure that out?"

"Not my first rodeo," replied Connie. "The universe is littered with custodians of extinct civilizations, and I think I've met most of them. Which makes me think that you've pulled me through time and space to tell me something helpful."

"Something like that," said the Custodian. "I don't know how much you understand, so please interrupt me if I tell you something you already know."

"No problem."

"My people created the caretaker force. Sort of. It was something of an accident, though a necessary one. You know about the Key, I assume."

"Manifestation of pure chaotic entropy," said Connie. "Or is there another?"

"No, that's the one. The Key, we didn't create. The Key came into existence shortly after the birth of creation. It drifted through the universe for untold eons, destroying planets, stars, burgeoning civilizations, whatever else it came across. We believe it was a remnant of whatever came before this universe, a piece of stubborn destructive nothingness.

"There was some debate over what to do with it. Some

suggested we ignore it, that given the vastness of the universe, it would be billions of years before it posed any serious threat. Others said we owed it to the lesser civilizations that would come after us to contain the Key. And some couldn't resist the Key and all the secrets of the cosmos it must have contained. It was a long debate, but ultimately, the choice was made to contain and study it."

She closed her eyes.

"It didn't go well for us."

"Rarely does," said Connie.

"Through science and engineering the likes of which this universe had never seen, we managed to capture the Key. It wasn't perfect. There was some incidental entropic leakage. We captured that as well. But there was always a little bit more. No matter how tightly we contained it, no matter how much we gathered, there was always more.

"And that's when we realized that it was impossible to contain it all. So we took that leakage and gathered it all together, and through science and trial and error and, honestly, a fair bit of luck, transformed it into something else: an entropy magnet."

She snapped her fingers.

"And it worked! It's hard to visualize, but all that loose chaotic decay gathered itself into a singular collection of negative potentiality. And the more entropy it drew, the more attractive it became. We suspected this would be a problem at some point, but it was less dangerous than the Key. And we figured we could solve that eventually."

"But you didn't," said Connie. "Or we wouldn't be having this conversation. What happened?"

The Custodian shrugged. "Time happened. Inevitability. Our great civilization rose and fell. Some think the Key hastened that. I say it was just the natural course of things. Either way, we faded away into memory and then into whispered legend and then into not even that. But before we did, we entrusted the Key to others to hide away, and we locked away the accumulated entropy of eons, never to be discovered.

"Except it was discovered by some curious explorers, and when they opened it up, the first thing it did was bond with one of them, taking them as its host. This host was driven by an insatiable need to seek out chaos and destruction and feed upon it. And that being, long since forgotten, was the first caretaker. Though that is a label that came much later. But that being was the first of a long line that leads directly to you."

Connie said, "I don't destroy the universe. I save it."

"Do you? You must know that the force within you was not always housed within so noble a host. The caretaker itself cares little for such labels. It is only drawn to entropy with an endless hunger. And its hosts are drawn to entropy to absorb it. Every disaster you've prevented, every life you've saved, every miraculous escape and last-minute reprieve has been an expression of that. A conscious and subconscious manipulation of order and probability to empower the force inside you.

"The caretaker mantle has been jumping from host to host to host for millennia. It's had more influence over some than others, but it uses whatever tools the host has to grow stronger. And you must be the strongest, the right host at the right time. Otherwise, you wouldn't be here."

"Right host and right time for what?"

"To destroy the universe," said the Custodian. "All that destructive potential hasn't gone away. It's still in you. But like a star reaching critical mass, you're about to explode. And all that delayed negative energy will flood the universe at once. And that will be the death knell of everything.

"Fortunately, we saw this coming, and we made one final preparation for correcting our mistake. My job is to implement that preparation. When the time is right, when the entropy attractor is near its peak capacity, I am to draw it here and free it from the host. The resulting destructive energy will only destroy a universe already dead."

"But what about the Key?" asked Connie.

"The Key will continue to exist, speeding the decay of the cosmos, but if we're talking on a timescale of the universe, it's relatively minor. Two or three billion years off the end. Those aren't even the good years."

"And what about all those people it hurts?"

"What are a few quadrillion lives, a few worlds, here or there? We're talking about the survival of the universe."

"No."

The Custodian's tongue flicked out of her mouth. "I'm sorry?"

"No. I'm not going to let that happen."

"Haven't you listened? There's a balance. The force inside you, it will destroy the universe at some point. But by letting it out here and now, we've prevented tragedy. And in a cosmic sense, it will balance out the damage the Key will do. So it's really the only solution."

"There's another way," said Connie.

The Custodian said, "I know it's not easy to hear, but—"

"There's another way. Send me back now, and I'll find it."

The Custodian stood, uncoiling her tail. "Your cooperation would've been appreciated, but it's not really necessary."

Connie pounced on the Custodian, lifting the short reptilian alien off her feet. "Send me back."

With a sweep of her tail, the Custodian knocked Connie's legs out from under her. She whipped the tail around Connie's neck and started choking her.

"Did you really think that just because I'm an enlightened superior being I won't resort to violence?" She lifted Connie in the air and slammed her back into the floor. "I don't know why we're bothering anyway. You wouldn't be here if you were already overflowing with destructive potential, waiting to be unleashed. All this conversation has been a consideration, a chance to explain the larger events you've been swept into. But soon it will all be over."

Connie fell limp. The Custodian released her and grabbed a pastry from the cart, nibbled at it.

"Oh, good. Jelly-filled. My favorite."

Connie grabbed the Custodian from behind and threw her to the floor. Connie grabbed a knife off the cart and used it to chop off the Custodian's tail in three hard swings. The severed limb flailed as the Custodian scrambled away.

"I can hold my breath a long time," said Connie.

"It's too late," grunted the Custodian with a smug grin.

Connie felt the gathered entropy within her rise. It boiled under her skin. She stumbled as it coursed out of her control, but she held it in.

"It'll be easier if you don't fight it," said the Custodian.

Connie retched as dizziness overcame her. The caretaker threatened to burst forth, and in that moment, she lost her grip on it. It slipped through her metaphysical fingers and destroyed the universe.

Or it should have.

It was too much to contain, but she didn't explode. She wrestled it down, focused herself. The caretaker settled into an uneasy churn in every one of her cells. But she could hold it. She could push past it.

The gathered entropy filled Connie, nauseating her, but also filling her with newfound strength. Too much strength. Too much power. It bristled under her skin, through her veins, straining to be free.

"That's not possible," said the Custodian.

"I do the impossible all the time," replied Connie, feeling simultaneously supercharged and exhausted at the same time.

The Custodian reached for her robe pocket. Connie grabbed her wrist.

"Relax. I'm just taking a reading."

Connie released her. The Custodian withdrew a small diagnostic robot. It hovered around Connie, scanning her.

"You're incomplete," said the Custodian. "Parts of the caretaker are missing."

"So what's that mean?"

"I don't know. It shouldn't even be possible. But I do know that even fractured, you can't hold this in forever."

"I can hold it in awhile longer," said Connie. "Long enough to figure something else out. Your civilization trapped the Key once, right? So let's trap it again."

"I'm telling you, the Key is unimportant."

"Show me how you did it," said Connie. "Let me try. And whether I succeed or fail, I'll come back here and die at the end of time."

"Why should I?"

"Because it's the only choice you have," she said. "If you really want to correct your mistake, then help me correct it."

"It won't work," said the Custodian.

"We're here at the end of time. The universe must not be destroyed by me in the past."

"That's not how time travel works," said the Custodian. "All futures are only potential futures. If I send you back, then you could very well erase this one."

"Okay, then how about this," said Connie. "You really don't have a choice. I can sense that the caretaker is strong enough to reverse whatever you used to pull me here. I'm going back, whether you like it or not. You owe it to the universe to at least give me a fighting chance."

The Custodian stepped over her severed, wiggling tail and offered Connie a small, silvery marble. The marble projected a holographic blueprint.

"It's not that difficult to build, if you have the right tools and expertise. But I should emphasize, it's only a temporary solution to a lesser problem."

Connie tucked the marble into her pocket. "Thank you."

The Custodian shrugged. "No scales off my tail. If I'm right, the moment you return to your proper point in space-time, I'll cease to exist. But I do have to observe that my people had ages to figure out this problem. What makes you think you can find a better solution?"

"Because it's what I do."

26

I thought Connie hated Kansas," said Byron.

" 'Hate' might be too strong a word," said Tia.

"I specifically remember her saying, 'I hate Kansas,' " said Byron. "More than once."

"Okay, so she's not crazy about it," admitted Tia. "But that's not her fault. Kansas has tried to kill her more than once."

"I feel like everyone and everything has tried to kill Connie at some point," said Byron.

"Not like Kansas," said Tia.

"Then why are we here?" he asked. "If Connie is bouncing around the universe, why would she choose to come here?"

"She's not choosing," said Tia. "She's being directed. Isn't that right?"

Bonita said, "Yes. But I still don't see how this will bring her to us."

"It's simple. Connie's out there, saving the universe. So we give her something to save."

Byron eyed the sign at the entrance of the Big Well Museum of Greensburg, Kansas. "And that something is here?"

"Are you going to come up with a better plan or just keep questioning mine?"

Byron shrugged. "Okay. You're in charge."

"How about you?" she asked Bonita.

Bonita held up her hands.

Chestnut sat in front of Tia and wagged her tail.

"Good," said Tia with a smile. "We have to hurry. They're almost closed."

She pushed open the door. Bonita followed. Byron told Chestnut to stay put.

"And try not to steal anything," he pleaded more than commanded.

She was already eyeing some tourists, but he had no time to waste.

Inside, Tia was being confronted by an employee.

"We won't be long, I swear," said Tia.

The employee shrugged, clearly not paid enough to have this argument.

"The Big Well is the largest hand-dug well in the world," explained Tia as she marched with purpose. "It was intended as a water source for the town. Or so the public record says. In fact, it was part of a plan to crack open an inter-dimensional portal and summon an alien god named Gug Kha Tuka-something something to our plane of existence."

"That's a mouthful," said Byron.

"Connie just calls it Gug. She first fought it when she was nine. Then when she was thirteen. Then again when she was eighteen. And a couple of times after that. I wasn't there for most of those fights, but she told me the stories."

They started down the staircase, going deeper into the well.

"You know Connie," she said. "It's hardly ever personal with her. But she hates Gug. Despises it. And if she can be anywhere in the universe, you can bet your ass she'll be here if it awakens again."

They reached the bottom of the spiral staircase and the well. There was nothing particularly menacing about it.

"Did you bring the thing?" asked Tia of Bonita.

Bonita pulled back her sleeve to expose a high-tech wrist device. She pushed a button on it, and an oddly shaped gizmo materialized in her palm. "One quantum destabilizer bomb. When this is activated, it'll blow a hole right through this dimension."

The silhouette of a museum employee leaned over the railing at the top of the well. "Folks, we're closing."

"Sure thing!" shouted back Tia. "We're almost done here."

Bonita knelt down, fiddling with the device.

"It has to be attuned. Otherwise, it's just a regular bomb, which won't do anyone any good."

"Maybe we shouldn't do this," said Byron.

"We've already talked about it," said Tia. "It's the only way to get Connie's attention."

"But I'm thinking about it, and if she is jumping throughout space, saving the universe, then wouldn't it make sense for her to already be here? Why would she have to wait until the last minute to stop us?"

"Because we haven't done it yet," said Tia.

"But we're going to do it. It'd be easier to stop us now."

"I don't know," said Tia. "Maybe there needs to be imminent danger."

"This danger feels pretty imminent."

"You're overthinking it," said Tia.

The bomb beeped twice. "It's done," said Bonita. She handed Tia a small trigger device. "Press this button for five seconds to detonate."

"Why am I detonating it?"

"Because it's your plan. I have enough blood on my hands. I'm not going to be responsible for the death of a solar system."

"Solar system? I thought this thing was only a threat to the planet," said Byron.

"Not from the readings I picked up," said Bonita.

Tia pocketed the detonator. "It'll be fine."

"You're starting to sound like Connie," said Byron.

"And she's always right," said Tia as they climbed the stairs.

"Yes, but she's Connie. We're us," he said. "We don't have her skills or knowledge."

"Which is all the more reason why she'll have to show up."

At the top of the well, the employees tried to hustle Tia, Byron, and Bonita out the door, but Tia resisted.

"Is the place empty yet?" she asked.

"Just you folks," said the guide.

"What about other employees?"

The guide frowned. "I'm going to have to ask you to leave now, miss, or I'm calling the police."

Bonita, sighing, summoned a blaster from her wrist-mounted materializer. She fired several sizzling shots into the ceiling. The employees froze.

"Oh, for the love of . . ." Bonita transformed into her true space cockroach form. She clicked her mandibles and fired off another few ceiling rounds. "Scram, already."

The employees all ran for the exits as Bonita dematerialized her weapon. "I should've just done that in the first place."

Tia pulled the detonator from her pocket and waited a few more moments for the area to clear. Then she pushed the button before she could talk herself out of it.

The quantum bomb exploded with the soft pop of a firecracker. Tia and Byron glanced down at the bottom of the well, where some wisps of smoke drifted upward.

"Well, shit," said Tia.

"Maybe that's why she didn't appear to stop us," said Byron. "She knew we'd fail."

A pinprick of light opened at the bottom of the well. It swirled into a larger vortex. A bit of green-gray slime bubbled out of the inter-dimensional breach, and the ancient god-thing Gug shrieked from its weakening prison.

"Well, shit," said Byron.

Gug pushed its amorphous tentacles into the universe, forcing its way through the breach.

Tia glanced around, expecting to see Connie any minute now.

"Where is she?" asked Byron.

"She'll be here," said Tia. "She'll be here."

She sounded less convinced the second time.

The god-thing pushed its misshapen head through the void. It glared with its dozen eyes, and its many mouths vomited acidic spit as it howled. It was like watching the well giving birth to the doom of the world. The malignant hate and rage radiated off Gug with a palpable heat.

It dug its claws into the well sides and pulled itself forth.

"Did we just destroy the universe?" asked Byron as he stepped away.

Bonita said, "No, just the solar system at best." Her wrist computer shrieked. "Maybe a galaxy."

"Why did you let me do this?" shouted Tia.

"You seemed like you knew what you were doing!" screamed Bonita over the gurgling wails of the god-thing.

"Why would I know what I'm doing? I'm just the stupid human!"

"What about all that talk about not nay-saying if we didn't have a better plan?"

"Well, I didn't think you'd let me destroy a galaxy!"

Bonita's wrist computer screeched. "Oh, well, that's pretty bad."

A giant hand thrust out of the hole, shattering the staircase. The god-thing rose from the well. Its squishy body broke apart and reassembled as it struggled to merge and corrupt this plane of existence. It glowered with its yellow, black, red, and purple eyes and howled. Cracks appeared in the walls and floor. The roof threatened to fall in. Gug's inhuman cries burrowed deep into the humans' minds, threatening to tear their sanity apart from the inside.

Chestnut came running in, barking furiously at Gug. Gug quieted, studied her with a confused, curious expression. Or maybe not. Byron ran over and grabbed her, pulling her away. Gug raised a hand, preparing to bring it down to crush both man and dog.

Connie materialized, decked in a long coat, carrying a strangely shaped cannon that she could barely hold in two hands. Gug paused, narrowed its many eyes.

"Connnnnn-stannnnnssss," it hissed.

She braced herself and unleashed a barrage from her weapon. The recoil pushed her back as the burner rounds seared Gug. The god-thing howled as it was rendered into a bubbling mound of jellied, fleshy goop. The slime burped as it began to regenerate itself.

The barrel of Connie's cannon burned red hot as it melted under its own heat. She dropped it and reached into her coat. "That was a bad idea."

"I told you it would work!" said Tia, smacking Bonita on the back. "Never had any doubt."

Connie pulled out a metallic disk and started pushing buttons on it. It rang melodiously with each touch.

"Where did you get a class nebula quantamic disintegrator?" asked Bonita.

"I know someone who knows someone who knows someone." She flicked a switch and the disintegrator made a low whirring sound. She smacked it twice, and it started to hum.

"Connie, we have to talk," said Tia.

"No time," said Connie. "I have to kill Gug once and for all and then land a jumbo jet in Norway and then save a sea monster from some poachers." She paused, looking far away as the universe whispered to her. "There's more to do."

"Connnnn-staaaaaansss," hissed Gug.

"Be right with you, buddy."

Byron said, "Connie, you can't keep doing this."

She looked at him, though it was like she was looking through him. "Sure I can."

She removed an ancient totem from her coat along with some duct tape. She used the tape to bind the totem and disintegrator together, then bit off the end with her teeth.

"You're going to want to step back," she said.

They did.

"About eighteen inches more," she said without looking at them.

Connie tossed her makeshift weapon into Gug. The god-thing's regenerating flesh grew around the device. Gug re-formed, growled and reached for her. Its arm disintegrated as lances of light punched through its unstable body at random angles. It convulsed, sinking into the well from whence it had spawned. Its angry rumbling shook the museum as Connie walked over to a soda machine. She used a sword to cut a hole in the machine. Cans came spilling out. She opened one and took a long, long drink.

"Is it dead?" asked Byron. The bestial noises echoing from the well made him think not.

"That is not dead which may eternal lie, but with a quantamic disintegrator and a Kandamian banishment artifact, even death may die." She put the can to her forehead and closed her eyes. "Give it a minute."

"Connnnn-stannnnssss," rumbled Gug.

The ground shook as a tower of light shot from the well and into the sky. Toxic purple goo splattered the ground, landing just a few inches from where Tia and Byron might have been standing. While they rubbed the blinding aftereffects from their eyes, Connie smashed the snack machine. She stuffed handfuls of candy bars into her pockets, opened one, and shoved half of it into her mouth.

"Starving," she explained with bulging cheeks. "Haven't had a chance to eat today. I think. I don't know. Hard to keep track of time."

Byron tried to brush a strand of hair stuck to her hand with dried blood. "You're hurt."

Chewing, she stepped away. "It's not my blood. Also, don't touch me."

"You can't keep this up," said Tia. "You're still human. You need to eat and sleep."

"No time." Connie crammed the rest of the candy bar into her mouth. "Do you have your Swiss Army knife on you, Byron?"

"Always," he said.

"I need it." Her expression went blank before snapping back. "I'll need it. After I land that plane."

"Sure, but can you spare a moment to just listen?"

She frowned. "Maybe a minute."

"Can you explain it better?" Tia asked Bonita.

"I'll try." Bonita's antennae twitched. "Connie, you're being overtaken by the caretaker mantle. This will kill you if you don't re-exert control. And if you die, then there will be nothing to stop Hiro from destroying the universe."

"I know."

"You know?" asked Tia.

Connie looked past her, a thousand yards into the distance at nothing. Nothing they could see, anyway. "I know, but I can't stop. The caretaker needs to be fed." She held out her hand. "Your knife, Byron."

"No," he said. "You can't have it. Not until we've talked about—"

She was on him, had him pinned to the floor before he even registered it. Tia and Bonita moved toward her.

"I wouldn't," Connie said.

She yanked the knife from his pocket.

The entropy rose within her. The museum cracked in

half. Rubble fell from the broken ceiling, and Tia almost fell into the chasm.

Connie staggered away from Byron. "Damn it. Shouldn't have touched you." She swallowed the power.

She was less a person, more an unstoppable force. But her eyes betrayed fatigue. She couldn't go on forever.

Chestnut nuzzled her hand. Smiling, Connie petted the dog, and she seemed more grounded.

"I'm still trying to figure it all out," she said. "But the caretaker is broken."

"We know," said Tia.

"No, you don't know," said Connie. "I think it's a good thing that it's broken. It's like I'm a bomb, but without the wires connected."

"That's good, right?" said Byron.

"Yes and no. I'm still a malfunctioning agent of destruction." She pointed at him. "And you're carrying the trigger. It's why I can't touch you."

"Your glorious death," he said.

"Our glorious death. The glorious death of everything." She shuddered, threatening to break apart at the seams. "Oh, this really sucks. I need you, Tia."

"But you said not to touch you," said Byron.

"No, I can't touch you. She's okay. She's good." Connie took Tia's hand and let some of the stored entropy flow between them. It knocked Tia on her ass, and she threw up.

"Sorry," said Connie. "I should've warned you."

Tia wiped the drool from her mouth. "What was that?"

"Just enough for you to carry," said Connie, helping Tia up. "Enough to buy me some more time. I can't give it to anyone else. It's only us. I can take some of it back if you can't handle it."

Tia waved her away. "No, I can do this if you need me to, whatever this is. But tell me you have a plan."

"I have a plan."

Smiling, she dropped the silver marble into Tia's hand.

"I have to go. You have maybe three days. Don't waste them."

She pointed to Byron. "Whatever you do, don't touch her, either."

Connie vanished.

Tia examined the marble. "I don't know what this is."

"I do." Bonita took the marble and twisted it delicately, and it projected holographic blueprints.

27

Patty had a helicopter pick them up and fly them out of Kansas and into Colorado's San Luis Valley. Over some unexceptional acreage of sand and brush, a secret entrance opened beneath them. The helicopter descended into the underground facility.

"You have an awful lot of secret bases for not a supervillain," observed Tia.

"It's not mine," said Patty. "I'm building it on spec for a client, but given the circumstances, I figured we could borrow it." The helicopter settled onto the landing pad as the entrance closed overhead. "But it is expensive, so try not to break anything."

On the pad, they were greeted by Reynolds and a team of contractors and engineers. Bonita, who had spent the flight studying the holographic schematics, pulled Reynolds aside and began conferring with him.

"Can they build it?" asked Byron.

"Let's hope so," said Patty.

"I wish Malady hadn't been blown up," said Tia. "I'd feel more confident if he were around."

Patty scanned some paperwork she was given. "You have to work with what you have, but I hire the best. If my team can build a moon base in three weeks, this machine in three days should be . . . well, not easy, but possible." She handed off the form. "In the meantime, you should get some rest."

"We can help," said Byron.

Patty said, "Oh, can you? Have a handy degree in theoretical quantum physics, do you?"

"Well, no, but—"

"Are you, by chance, some expert on electrical or mechanical engineering?"

"Well, no—"

"Can I be blunt? You are here, Byron, because we still believe it is your destiny to die saving the universe. And you, Mrs. Yukimura-Durodoye, are here simply as a courtesy. It is my job to manage my team, and your job to stay out of the way until we need you. If we even end up needing you. Have a snack. Get some rest. We'll call you if . . ."

Her voice trailed off as she walked away.

"Something to eat does sound good," said Byron.

Chestnut barked.

"Come on, then," said Tia. "Commissary is this way."

"How do you know that?"

"I've seen a lot of secret lairs. You get a feel for their layouts."

She led them through the base. Construction was almost done on this one. The logos had yet to be stenciled. Many of the labs were bare-bones, waiting for whatever fiendish scientific experiment the final owner would want to plug into them. Security systems were being wired in. But if Tia imagined the construction crews in matching jumpsuits, it wasn't hard to see what it would end up being.

The commissary was bustling. After a short wait in line, they had servings of mac 'n' cheese and steamed veggies plopped on their trays. They found an empty table in the hall. Byron took a bite of the macaroni. It wasn't bad.

He was about to offer a spoonful to Chestnut, but she was content munching on a tray of meat loaf she'd gotten somewhere during the walk from the line to the table.

"What did Connie do to you?" asked Byron.

Tia picked at her food. "She put more of the caretaker in me." She nibbled at some macaroni, but she was still feeling ill. She dabbed at the sweat on her forehead. "I can handle it."

"I wish she could've told us her plan."

"Byron, I've spent decades getting in and out of perilous situations with Connie. It isn't our job to know the plan. It's our job to be ready when the plan happens. I know it stinks, but we'll get through it. We'll get Hiro and Connie back."

She reached across the table and put her hand on his. A jolt ran between them, and the commissary lights flickered. Chestnut latched onto Byron's belt and yanked him back.

"Oh, right," she said. "No touching."

"So where is Hiro?" asked Byron. "We know Connie is out there, doing her thing, saving the world. What about Hiro?"

"It's a good question. If he's the anti-Connie, then maybe he's out there, sowing chaos and disaster."

"So why isn't he here? If he's the anti-Connie, and she appeared when we imperiled the world, wouldn't he sense what we're doing? Wouldn't he try to stop us if it could work?"

"Damn, I hadn't thought of that," said Tia. "But maybe he hasn't noticed."

"Maybe. Or maybe we're just wasting our time."

"No," said Tia. "It's Connie's plan, and I don't know what it is, but I have to believe it's going to work." She pushed away from the table. "And we're going to help make it work."

They marched through the base for half an hour before they could finally find someone to give them directions to Patty's office.

"We can be useful," said Tia.

Patty smirked. "I'm sure you can. If you could build a"— she flipped through some paperwork—"lepton phase array, it'd really help me out. All my sources are coming up empty."

"I might know someone," said Tia, dialing her phone. "Hey, Larry. This is Tia. I was wondering if you have any lepton phase arrays lying around? You'll check? Thanks."

She lowered the phone.

"He's checking."

Tia snapped her fingers at Patty, who reluctantly handed over Reynolds's hard-to-find parts list.

"You do? Two of them? Great. I don't suppose you'd mind letting us borrow one? I wouldn't ask if it wasn't important. That's terrific. You're a lifesaver. While I have you on the phone, mind if I ask about a few other things?"

She walked away, leaving Byron and Chestnut standing there.

Patty asked, "Don't suppose your dog has a talent for electrical engineering?"

Three days later, the final pieces of the machine were being assembled. The machine took up most of the lab. It looked pretty much identical to any other feat of engineered superscience.

"Is it working?" asked Tia.

"We don't know," said Bonita. "We haven't turned it on yet."

"What are we waiting for?" asked Byron.

Bonita said, "I know you're impatient, but it won't do any good if we rush it. We'll only get one shot at activating this . . . whatever it is."

"You don't know what it does?" asked Tia.

"The nearest answer I could give you is that it breaks the laws of physics. If it works."

"It'll work," said Reynolds.

Tia wiped at her nose, noticing some blood on her hand. The nosebleeds had become a problem seven hours ago. She could feel her body breaking down. If she touched Byron now, the chaos within her would destroy her and everything within miles. Maybe farther than that.

Maybe much farther.

She took a cautious step away from him, even though she was already well out of arm's reach. Couldn't hurt to be safe.

"I know that I'm falling apart," said Tia. "Connie has to be a hundred times worse."

The last bits of machinery were locked into place. Reynolds gave the signal, and the device hummed to life. It didn't melt or explode, which everyone took as a good sign.

"Never had any doubts," said Patty. "I only hire the best."

"Now what?" asked Tia.

Bonita flipped a few small switches, and the machine's hum pitched a few octaves higher. Her hand hovered over the final activation button.

28

Somewhere in the vast universe, a planet-killer asteroid was on a collision course with the Xorlinian home world. Connie sat on the bridge of a spaceship, watching the asteroid hurtle past.

The Xorlinian crew lay unconscious at their stations. A sudden malfunction in the atmosphere recyclers had pumped out too much oxygen, though it was a little thin for a human. The ship's gravity beam was primed and ready to fire. The helm operator's hand was right next to the blinking button.

A push of the button would be all it would take. The beam would divert the asteroid, allowing it to miss the home world by a bare 17,000 miles. But that window was closing.

She hadn't pushed the button yet, though.

"Having second thoughts?" said Hiro.

Connie didn't jump. It wasn't in her nature. And she'd sensed his arrival. They were bound together by the shared force within them.

"You can talk now?" asked Connie.

He pushed a Xorlinian out of his chair and had a seat. "Why don't you do it? Why would the fabled Constance Verity hesitate to save untold lives with one simple press?"

He grinned.

"Is it because you're so full of negative potentiality that you can barely hold it in as it is? Is it because the lives of a few billion souls that you'll never even meet is a price you're willing to pay to buy this doomed universe a few more minutes?"

"Fuck off," she said.

She pressed the button. The gravity beam diverted the asteroid's course.

The averted chaos channeled into her. She closed her eyes and pushed it down. She was a bomb without a detonator, but still dangerously unstable. A momentary slip might be all it would take to jostle her into exploding.

"The longer you go, the worse it will be," said Hiro.

She ignored him, went to check on the recyclers. It was nothing serious. She could fix it. She undid the coupling and inserted a new scrubber from the spares. The recycler hummed back into full operation, and the oxygen levels fell.

Under normal circumstances, she could handle these levels for a few minutes, but she was on the verge of exhaustion. What little energy she did have was devoted to keeping the caretaker essence from exploding with her.

She checked on the crew. The Xorlinians were stirring.

"You can't stop it, can you?" asked Hiro. "Always have to save people."

"Shut up." It wasn't her wittiest retort, but she was barely holding together.

She helped the captain to a seat. "The asteroid—" he said.

"Taken care of," she said.

He blinked his four eyes and wiggled his long snout in a gesture of thanks. "We owe you untold gratitude."

"It's cool," she rasped. She leaned against a console and closed her eyes. "Just need a moment to clear . . . my head."

She listened to the universe, to the numberless disasters and tragedies, great and small, occurring now. It was too much.

But she could handle one or two more. A small one.

She blinked across space. The transition was smoother and faster. Not even a touch of disorientation as she appeared in the office. She pushed her way past the office workers to the view of a dangling window washer. She cleared her head enough to use a one-inch punch to shatter the glass. She pulled the washer in just as his harness snapped.

"Oh God. Thank you," he said.

She ignored the applause, grabbing a cup of coffee out of someone's hand. She gulped it down and sat in a chair.

Hiro poked his head over a cubicle. "I've been busy myself. Pushed a guy into traffic today who would've prevented World War III in twenty years. And dropped an air-conditioning unit on somebody's head. Just for a laugh."

She ignored him.

She could hold more. Just a little more.

She slipped away, landing in front of a kid standing over an anthill with a magnifying glass. She blocked the sun with her shadow.

"Hey, what gives, lady?" he asked.

"Beat it, kid."

Hiro laughed. "Is this what you've been reduced to? Saving insects?"

"It all counts," she said.

"You don't honestly believe that, do you?" He knelt down beside the anthill. "You have to feel it now. All the chaos and decay around you, all the time. A universe crumbling one atom at a time." He raised a fist over the hill with a devilish smile. "This isn't any different than this world. No harder to crush."

He lowered his hand.

"Not that I need to. It's falling apart well enough on its own."

"Then why are you here?" she asked. "If it's all pointless, then isn't destroying it pointless?"

He wagged his finger. "You got me there. It's just . . . well, it's just that it bugs the ever-loving shit out of me. What can I say? It's just my nature."

He pulled his foot back to kick the anthill.

Connie jumped on him, grabbing him by the arms.

"It's not going to work," he said.

She slipped free of the world, dragging him along with

her, appearing in the middle of the lab. Hiro's derisive laughter echoed through the lab. Connie squeezed Hiro in a bear hug, anchoring him in time and space. But she could feel him slipping free.

"Now," said Connie.

Bonita threw the switch, and the machine sprang to life. The containment sphere shimmered as it drew the entity's otherworldly energies into it.

"Is this your master plan?" asked Hiro through clenched teeth. "You can't put me back. I won't let you."

He tried teleporting away, but the machine anchored him.

Hiro screamed as the thing fought to remain in him. His skin turned ashen. His eyes yellowed.

"I'll tear him apart! I'll do it! There will be nothing left. Not even a single goddamn memory."

Tia took a step toward them.

"I've got this!" said Connie.

She pulled him closer. Parts of his skin had fallen away to reveal the muscle and bone underneath.

She whispered, "I know you're still in there, Hiro. And I know there's nothing you can't escape from, no prison that can hold you. Show us what you can do and get out of this one."

Hiro stopped yelling. A confused expression crossed his face.

"You've got a wife now, you idiot. Don't leave behind the one commitment you've made in your life."

He looked to Tia.

And he smiled.

Connie wrapped him in her arms and held tight as the
entity drained from his body. Its disembodied screams echoed
through the portal.

He fell limp. She lowered him to the floor as Tia and
Byron came running over. Hiro was in one piece, more or
less. A few patches of skin were gone. Some of his hair. A few
fingernails. A finger.

"That really sucked," he said.

But he was smiling.

Tia kissed him as Connie stood to one side.

"Closing the portal," said Reynolds, throwing a switch.

The machine fizzled as the other-dimensional pinprick
shrank, but wouldn't close.

"It's not working," said Bonita.

The portal widened. A trail of lights connected from it to
Connie, Tia, and Byron.

"We're still tethered to it," she said. "As long as the caretaker is on this side, it will find its way back."

Shrieking, the thing on the other side pushed its way into
reality. Its presence, either by accident or intention, caused
part of the giant containment machine to catch fire.

"It's not going to hold!" shouted Reynolds. "Whatever you
plan on doing, do it now!"

Byron stepped up. "I know what I have to do. I have to
die so the universe lives."

"No, you don't," said Connie.

"It's okay." He smiled with quiet acceptance of his fate. "It isn't ideal, but someone has to do it. A plan millions of years in the making. We can't just change it now."

The other-dimensional tear widened.

"Nobody dies, Byron," she said. "I've got a better plan."

"So what do we do?" asked Tia.

Connie hugged Tia, taking back all the caretaker mantle. Connie crackled with power. Too much to contain, but unable to release it. Her body started breaking down, held together only through sheer willpower.

She looked to Byron and the thread of energy connecting them. He was too close. Another step closer could spell disaster.

"I love you," she said, fighting back the destructive potential consuming her from the inside. "If this doesn't work . . ."

"Connie, I—"

"Nobody dies," she said. "Keep the door open for me."

She jumped into the portal. It swallowed her, and the machine quieted. Technicians ran about putting out fires.

"Is that it?" asked Patty.

"Still getting questionable readings," said Reynolds.

"It's subdued, but the Key is still not contained," said Bonita.

The portal, now a small point of light, hovered before them. Glittering particles of negativity connected Byron and Tia to it.

29

The universe fell away from Connie, and there was only emptiness. She plummeted forever or only a moment until she finally just stopped. There was no sense of impact, but she lay on a metallic floor.

The Custodian stood over her.

"Well, you blew it."

The Custodian offered Connie a hand up. She stood once again at the end of time.

"You didn't think it would be that simple, did you?" asked the Custodian. "Just shove the Key back into its box, as if it would all reset?"

"No, I didn't," said Connie. "But it was the best plan I had."

"Hardly a plan." The Custodian stood before the window and stared at the dying light of the final star. "But I told you it wouldn't work."

"Had to try."

"Yes, I suppose you did." The Custodian's lips curled into a smile. "And it's laudable in a way. That never-say-die attitude carried you far. No wonder you're the greatest of the hosts. You have just the right combination of foolish determination and optimistic arrogance. But it's over now. You had your shot. But it was always going to end here with you and me."

"Yes, it was." Connie walked over to the dessert cart and picked up a donut. She took a bite.

"So you accept it, then," said the Custodian. "For the good of the universe, you will finally unleash all that oblivion stored within you."

Connie laughed.

"Something amusing?" asked the Custodian.

"You must think I'm really stupid," said Connie.

"I do, but what does that have to do with anything?"

"You're not the Custodian. This is not the end of time. And these are not donuts." She dropped her pastry on the dessert cart. "It's not even convincing. Sure, it looks the part, but nothing feels real. The donuts don't have any taste. I can't feel the floor under my feet."

The room dissolved, replaced by an empty white expanse. A generic version of nothingness. Connie had seen actual nothingness, and it was less interesting than this.

The Custodian become a faceless thing, a mass of swirling colors with a single, twinkling light in its center. "So you figured it out. So what?"

"You're the Key," she said.

"The Key was a doorway into your universe. I'm something

greater, though I'm not really anything you can comprehend," it replied. "I only look like this now because your mind has given me form. I'm the beginning. Before there was anything, there was me: the foundation of all reality, of all possibilities."

Connie's vision cleared. The Foundation took on a more solid shape. Its single eye became two. A mouth formed, and it smiled.

"Care for a tour?" It gestured. "That is nowhere. And over here, more nothing. And over there . . ." It paused. "Say, that's new."

A rip in the void hovered over their heads. It was either a million miles away or within touching distance. Space was a mutable concept here.

"I have to admit, you're fighting this with everything you have. I suppose you think you've managed it, some glorious sacrifice, sending yourself into this empty void to save the universe. But you've actually managed to make it worse for yourself. Outside of here, you would've only destroyed your universe. But here you'll destroy everything, bring it all crashing down. Why do you think I let you build your portal machine? I could've stopped it at any point, but this made my job a lot easier."

It plucked the light strands connecting Connie to the rip. The connection vibrated like a guitar string throughout Connie's body, and she could feel the universe echoing back.

The Foundation, vaguely humanoid, whirled on her. Its simulated body twisted in inhuman ways and when it walked, its legs flopped like rubber.

"All that power within, waiting to come out. You might as well let it out now. Why suffer needlessly?"

"Oh, shut up."

She punched it in its face-like protrusion. The lack of physical feedback made the act unsatisfying. The head popped, and the Foundation collapsed into a black-and-blue puddle, only to re-form a moment later.

"You can't fight your way out of this," it said. "You're out of daring escapes. It's finally caught up to you. There's only the end."

"You sure like to talk for a thing that doesn't really exist," said Connie.

The Foundation shrugged. "I've spent eternity as a formless hunger for oblivion. Let me enjoy myself while I can.

"You, however, still deny the obvious. I'm not a villain you can defeat with some last-minute daring risk. I transcend time and space and the concept of existence itself. When the multiverse is gone, when everything has vanished without a trace, I'll be the last thing left behind in the blessed silence."

It continued to refine itself. The edges of its body sharpened. It was still a concept wrapped in an unconvincing shell. It pointed to the portal connecting Connie to the universe, which had taken on the appearance of an actual door. The Foundation put its head against the door and listened for a moment.

"And this is the universe. Worlds quietly crumble away. Lives come and go. An endless cycle of death and rebirth."

It stuck a tonguelike thing from its mouthlike thing.

"I mean, gross, right? All that matter and energy colliding with itself. What a racket! What a fucking mess. No one will miss it when it's gone."

An endless procession of doors materialized around them, stretching into eternity. Each one connected to another world, another universe.

The Foundation, almost completely humanoid, turned to her. Its skin was pale and waxy and its milky eyes never blinked. And when it talked, its mouth moved but the voice came from everywhere, since they were really inside it.

"You look like you're holding in a lot. Let me help you with that."

It put a hand on her shoulder. The entropy rose in Connie. Her body burst opened as all the destructive potential gathered by her and every caretaker before her unleashed itself. The Foundation crumbled, and all the infinite universes stacked delicately upon it came crashing down.

The end to all things.

It was, without a doubt, the final and most glorious death there would ever be.

Except it didn't happen.

The entropy gathered back into Connie. It was all too much to bear out in the real world. But here, in a place that didn't exist, it wasn't that hard. She swallowed it all down with a smile.

The Foundation was flummoxed. "How? You're only flesh and blood."

"What's flesh and blood here?" asked Connie. "You said it yourself. This place is nothing."

"But you're not. You shouldn't be able to contain the caretaker essence."

"You're right." Energy crackled along Connie's skin, swam through her veins, sizzled at her fingertips. It kind of tickled. "But I'm not carrying all the caretaker. I left a little bit of it behind."

"Your death," it said.

"I'm a bomb without a detonator," said Connie.

"I suppose this was your plan all along. A noble sacrifice, just the two of us bound together in this emptiness for eternity?"

"No, not quite." She sat, though it was more like floating here.

The destructive potentiality rumbled within. She rode it like a wave. It slipped from her control. It would've overwhelmed her anywhere else. But here there was no one to save and nothing else to add to it. And without that small, most vital piece of the caretaker in the universe just next door, the entropy slid across this emptiness before sliding back into her.

The Foundation glowered. Its human shape drifted apart. It wrapped itself around her, an oppressive cloud.

She hummed "Come On Eileen" and ignored it. It was a nice song.

If this was it, she could live with that. It was a weird version of a glorious death, but it wasn't so bad.

But this wasn't it.

"I'll go back," said the Foundation. "The way is still open. And with you here, nothing can stop me. It won't be as efficient, but I'll still get the job done, one universe at a time if necessary."

It moved toward the door, but it never drew any closer.

"What is distance in this place?" she asked, a smile on her lips.

"This is my domain," the Foundation growled.

"Our domain," she corrected. "You might as well get used to sharing it."

"You are not more powerful than me."

"I'm brimming with destructive potential. If I were to step through any of these doors, I'd destroy the universe on the other side. Whereas you'd have to start all over. Which of us embodies ultimate inescapable oblivion better?"

Screaming, the Foundation pounced on Connie. Or it tried to. It never reached her, just hung suspended, its limbs flailing.

"You'll just wear yourself out," said Connie. "This will go a lot smoother for you if you accept that this is how it is."

The Foundation became a shrieking, writhing blob as it struggled ineffectively.

"Have it your way," Connie said. "You'll figure it out. Eventually."

The Foundation quieted. Its body congealed with cracked skin and hollow eyes.

"Fine," it said churlishly. "But even if you don't explode with all that power, it still isn't in your control. It will eat away at this realm slowly. Might take a little while longer, but I can wait."

"I don't think I'll be sticking around that long. I'm already bored," admitted Connie. "Hazard of the life I've lived, the life you gave me."

The door to her universe was flung open and spat out Tia. She screamed, careening in a free fall of her own mind until she noticed Connie sitting there.

"Oh, hey," said Connie.

She took Tia's hand as Tia set her feet down on the non-ground.

"This is weird," said Tia.

"What are you doing here?" asked Connie.

"I came for you. Byron's holding the door open."

"I don't know how you did it," said Connie. "I took the caretaker out of you."

"I think there's a little bit left," said Tia. "I can feel it. Enough to let me through at least."

The Foundation, shapeless, slithered around them, cackling. "You're a fool. Now that you're here, I'm going to use you against—"

"Shut up," said Connie, punching the Foundation again, causing it to crumble into a ball of shapeless lights again.

"Oh God," said Tia. "I didn't even think about that."

"It's fine," said Connie. "It's already over. Actually, I'm

glad you're here. You were here with me when the caretaker mantle first kicked in. You should be here when I finally see it through."

The Foundation, hoping Connie was distracted, slipped toward the door. She stepped on one of its tendrils, and it scrambled and clawed futilely, growling and hissing.

"I'll tear your universe apart atom by atom!"

"What's his deal?" asked Tia.

"Just ignore him. He is right, though. Even with Byron holding the trigger, I can't contain it forever." Connie clenched her fist and sparks of entropy drifted off her hand, burning at the Foundation. The damage was minor, but it would do the job eventually.

"Then what's the plan?" asked Tia.

Connie grinned. "Glad you asked. See, this whole caretaker gig, it was never meant to save the world. It's inevitable that it will eventually destroy the universe, but it doesn't have to do it all at once. It's just a question of how to get rid of it without doing that."

Hundreds of doors appeared around them. Thousands. Countless infinite doorways to countless infinite universes. All delicately balanced on the Foundation.

She put a finger on one of those doors. A bit of raging negative potential slipped from her. Anywhere else, it would've been a flood, but here, she could control it just enough.

"In that universe, everyone's shoes just came untied at once," she said.

She touched another door. "In this one, a meteor collides with a dead planet."

She pointed toward a third door, not even having to touch it now that she was getting the hang of it. "Misplaced keys, forgotten telephone numbers."

The Foundation growled. "Oh, you think you're so fucking clever, don't you."

"Quiet. I'm trying to concentrate." She strolled down the infinite worlds, leaving little specks of chaos in her wake.

"A spaceship's hyperdrive doesn't work for thirty seconds," she said. "A star nobody notices burns out a million years ahead of schedule. Some people's allergies act up." Smiling, she paused at one. "Somebody trips. But nobody dies. No irreversible tragedies. Just some minor misfortunes and troublesome inconveniences and a planet or two nobody will notice is gone."

The Foundation said, "You think this will work? You're only delaying the inevitable, planting my seeds of destruction in all those other universes."

"Can't be helped," said Connie.

"You can't save them all."

The harmless packets of magnetic entropy floated through the cosmos, finding new hosts, creating new caretakers. Dozens of them. Hundreds. Thousands. The power drained from her in waves and in an instant, because what was time in this place?

"There will always be a caretaker," she said. "It doesn't have to be me."

When it was all gone, she realized there was a little bit left. There would always be a little bit left. Enough to bend the odds in her favor. Enough to help her save the world.

The Foundation screamed. "This isn't the end of it! You're only a temporary bit of matter with delusions of grandeur, but I'm forever. I'll always be here. I'll win eventually!"

"Maybe, but not today."

She opened the door to her universe. "Come on, Tia. We're done here."

The Foundation howled at them, tried to follow, but there wasn't enough caretaker essence left in any of them to keep the portal open. It shut the moment they were through. And with a final powerless rage, the door collapsed into a small crystal sphere that rolled across the lab's floor.

Connie picked up the Key. There would always be a Key, and there would always be someone to stop it from destroying the universe.

"Did we win?" asked Byron.

She threw her arms around him. He tensed, but there was no feedback, no threatening apocalyptic release.

The wall burst apart as a mech suit punched its way into the lab. The towering robotic exoskeleton tromped over and aimed its many guns at Connie.

Blog's voice blared from the mech suit. "Constance Verity, for the good of the universe, you must die!"

His many weapons hummed as they powered up. Before he could attack, a shrill ping sounded.

"One second. I need to take this."

Blog lowered his guns.

"Yes, I have her right here," he said. "Definitely no way she can escape. Well, yes, I know she's escaped before, but she's—what? Are you sure about that? Because I'm not going to get a better chance than right now. Well, don't yell at me. I'm just double-checking."

The mech suit powered down. Its chest cavity opened, and the diminutive alien stepped out.

"So even though it wasn't my idea in the first place, and I didn't volunteer for this job, I've still been told to offer my apologies for any inconvenience I might have caused."

"Apology accepted," said Connie.

30

With no one trying to kill her and no longer plugged into the chaotic universe, Connie allowed herself to sit and catch her breath. She flopped into a folding chair while Patty's crew cleaned up the mess.

"What do we do with this?" asked Tia, holding the Key.

"I'll take it," said Bonita. "I can build a containment unit, and it's too dangerous to be trusted in human hands. No offense."

"Didn't your civilization build an evil god-computer?" asked Tia.

"Oh, just let her have it," said Connie.

Bonita tucked the crystal orb into a pouch. "I appreciate your faith."

"Sure. Also, you'll know where to find me if you screw up."

Bonita's antennae straightened in offense, but then she laughed. "Yes, Connie, I am relieved to know that I will."

She pushed a button on her belt and transmitted away in a flash.

Patty said, "I told you we were on the same side."

"Except you almost did the exact wrong thing," said Tia. "If you'd had your way, Byron would've sacrificed himself and destroyed the universe in the process."

"Mistakes were made, but ultimately, it all worked out. And you couldn't have done any of this without my resources or Reynolds's genius."

"Can I punch her again?" asked Tia.

Connie petted Chestnut. "Go ahead. I'm too tired to stop you even if I wanted to."

Hiro spoke up from behind Tia. "She's not worth it, baby."

Tia jumped. "You shouldn't be standing."

"I'm fine." He disappeared behind a puff of smoke. When the smoke cleared, he was still there, coughing. He braced himself against Tia. "Okay, maybe I could use a day or two of bed rest."

Connie let Byron help her to her feet. It was good that they could touch again without risking destroying the universe.

"So I still have that piece of caretaker in me?" he asked.

"You can't really get rid of it," she said.

"Does that mean I'm still destined to die a glorious death?"

"I don't think so," she said. "The death clause was an expression of the caretaker's destructive potential. Now that it's been drained off, it's deactivated. Not gone, but not really a threat anymore. I was a bomb without a detonator. Now you're a detonator without a bomb."

"And that's safe?"

"Safer," she said. "I can't make any promises, but it's not dangerous right now."

Reynolds approached. "I could probably remove the care-taker fragment from you, Mr. Bowen."

"No, thanks," said Byron.

Reynolds said, "I would expect you'd like to get rid of it."

"If it's not dangerous, then what's it matter?" asked Byron. "And it's better if Connie is around to keep an eye on it if it is."

"We agree on that," said Reynolds. "It was a pleasure working with you, Ms. Verity."

"Please, call me Connie," she said. "You're a hell of an engineer, Reynolds."

"Thanks . . . Connie."

She asked, "Ever thought about being a good genius?"

"Well, I'll admit that there are times I wish my research was applied toward more productive ends."

"Call me next week," she said. "I'll put you in touch with some people."

"Now, just a minute," said Patty. "You can't poach my people after I helped you save the universe."

"You're lucky I don't do worse," said Connie. "But you did end up helping more than you hurt, so I'm feeling charitable."

She leaned into Byron. "Now let's go home already. I want to crawl into bed and not get out for a week."

And she did just that.

31

After destroying and / or saving the universe, things calmed down a bit. There were still disasters to be prevented, evil to be thwarted, and adventures to be had, but it all seemed more relaxed. Connie was still busy though, and it was four weeks before she found the opportunity to return the Strand of Hemsut to Shai. She offered the strand to Shai. "Thanks for this."

Shai took the strand. "My pleasure."

"Hope I'm not like looking into the sun anymore."

The goddess of destiny shook her head. She closed the door, but Connie stopped it from shutting all the way with a gentle hand.

"So did I do what I was supposed to do?" she asked.

"You destroyed the universe, didn't you? Just very slowly."

"Seems like kind of a cop-out."

"Take it up with fate." Shai, half-visible through the cracked door, smiled enigmatically. "I'm retired."

—

"I don't have to go," said Tia.

"Go," said Connie. "You've put this off long enough. It'll be fine."

"But what if something happens?" asked Tia.

Hiro peeked from the other side of the Manta Ray, where he and Byron were loading luggage.

"Nothing is going to happen, honey."

Tia looked doubtful.

"Nothing is going to happen that I can't handle," said Connie.

"And she has Byron," added Hiro, tossing in a suitcase.

"And Chestnut," said Connie, petting the dog beside her.

Tia said, "Well . . . if Chestnut is around . . . ."

"You have to go on your honeymoon sometime," said Connie.

"What about my double honeymoon idea?" asked Tia.

She'd been pitching that ever since Connie and Byron had quietly tied the knot in a civil ceremony a few weeks ago. They'd agreed anything more elaborate was asking for trouble. Connie had already ruined two wedding receptions. She didn't need a third on her record.

"Just go. Have fun." Connie pulled Tia in for a hug.

"Okay, but you promise that you'll call me if anything serious happens," said Tia.

"I promise," said Connie. "Now get out of here. Before Hiro decides to leave without you."

Hiro, suddenly beside her, said, "I'll do it too."

Byron closed the compartment and gave it a tap with his knuckles. "All set."

"Pardon the interruption," said Automatica. "I made sandwiches and snacks for your flight. They are already in the mini-fridge."

"That's very considerate of you," said Tia.

Doctor Malady stepped from behind his robot bride. "Consider it an apology for my weather machine malfunction at your reception and my bride's unfortunate malfunction."

"That wasn't really your fault, Doc," said Connie. "Just as long as we're cool again, Auto."

Automatica studied Connie for a moment. "No imminent threat detected."

Malady said, "Then call it a gift to the happy newlyweds."

Tia kissed the mad genius's wrinkled forehead. "Thank you, you old romantic."

He blushed. "My pleasure. I do love love."

"It is statistically significant when compatible relationships are achieved," said Automatica.

"Stop." Malady adjusted his monocle. "You'll make me cry."

Tia and Hiro boarded the Ray.

"The flight coordinates are already programmed in," said Malady. "Just push the button labeled GO."

"So long, suckers." Hiro reached for the button, but Tia stopped him.

"You'll tell me how the thing goes, right?" she asked Connie and Byron.

"We'll tell you," said Byron, putting his arm around Connie.

Hiro jabbed the button. The Ray's canopy sealed itself as

it rose into the sky. It turned toward the direction of Hawaii and shot over the skyline, disappearing in seconds.

"Thanks for letting us borrow the Ray," said Connie.

Malady said, "What's the point of engineering a supersonic flying submersible if you can't lend it to a friend now and then?"

Automatica took his hand, and together, the short mad genius and seven-foot robot walked toward the condo.

"Is it weird that I think they're a cute couple?" asked Byron.

Connie kissed him. "Whatever works, right?"

"How do you think he survived that lab explosion?"

"Who knows? My bet is on cloning."

Her phone beeped, and her first instinct was that an emergency had sprung up. But it was just her reminder. Not that she needed reminding.

"Are you ready for this?" he asked.

"I'm ready."

Mrs. Shelly at the adoption agency was a round little woman who always wore pink and walked in a perpetual hurry. Her heels clicked with an intensity that made even Connie a little on edge. Aside from that, she was a lovely woman who simply didn't have time for nonsense.

She click-click-clicked her way down the hallway, flipping through the paperwork on her clipboard. Connie and Byron followed along, though it was more like being pulled in her wake.

"That letter of recommendation is from the president

of the UN," said Connie, sounding more nervous than she expected. "And that one is from the chancellor of Beta-Prime. It's a utopian world."

Mrs. Shelly let her clipboard fall to her side. "Mrs. Verity, Mr. Bowen, I'm not interested in how many important people you know. The only person I care about at this moment is on the other side of this door."

She put her hand on the handle.

"I'm sure you're very impressive. And you seem like a lovely couple. But this isn't about you."

"No, ma'am," said Connie. "Yes, ma'am."

Mrs. Shelly opened the door and stepped aside. Her heels click-click-clicked as she disappeared down the hall.

Byron squeezed Connie's hand, and she felt better. Not relaxed. But better.

They entered. A ten-year-old girl stood in the back, tapping her fingernails against a fire extinguisher on the wall. She glanced at them.

"Hey," she said.

"Hi," said Connie. "Are you Rikki?"

The girl looked at her funny. Because it was a stupid question. Of course she was Rikki.

"My friends call me Risky."

"That's fun," said Byron.

She shrugged. "I guess."

Connie and Byron had a seat at the table in the center of the room. Risky shuffled over and joined them.

"I know you," she said. "You're famous, aren't you?"

"Kind of," said Connie.

"I don't know you," she said to Byron.

"Yeah, I'm not famous," he admitted apologetically.

"It's no big deal."

Connie said, "This is weird, isn't it?"

"Weird for you," said Risky. "Not me."

Connie didn't know what to say. She hoped Byron would step in, but he was as awkward as her. Risky put her head on the table.

"I've been to the moon," Connie blurted out.

"That's cool," said Risky, unimpressed.

"I know kung fu."

"Neat."

Connie pulled out her cell. "Do you want to talk to Dracula? I can call him."

Risky waved her off, stared at the table. "No, thanks."

An alien sensation gripped Connie. Panic. She'd forgotten what it felt like. After everything she'd done, she was being defeated by a girl's indifference.

"We have a dog," said Byron.

Risky perked up. "What kind?"

"Golden retriever," he said. "Her name is Chestnut. She's a wonder dog."

Risky sat up in her chair. "Chestnut's kind of a dumb name."

"We didn't name her," said Connie.

"That's cool." A brief pause. "Dogs are cool. I like dogs. So are you rich?"

"Yes."

"Like mansion rich? Butler rich?" Risky mimed drinking a cup of tea with her pinkie out. "Cotillion rich?"

"No mansion. No butler," said Connie.

"I've never been to a cotillion," said Byron.

"I have," said Connie. "They're overrated."

Mrs. Shelly opened the door and stuck her head into the room. "Mrs. Verity, there's some paperwork I need you to sign. Won't take a moment."

Connie stood, placing her hand on Byron's shoulder. "You stay. Talk. I'll be back."

She joined Mrs. Shelly.

"She seems like a good kid," said Connie.

"Oh, yes, wonderful," said Mrs. Shelly. "Sometimes a little distracted and prone to flights of fancy. Would you believe she thinks Mr. Pliskin, our janitor, is planning to rule the world with some ancient forbidden relic?"

Connie chuckled. "That's funny."

"Yes, she has quite the little story about it. Claims he's digging a tunnel in the cleaning supplies closet into a forgotten temple of Mu. Have you ever heard of such a thing? Very elaborate. If you ask her about it, she can give you all these marvelous details."

"Can she?"

A. LEE MARTINEZ

Connie signed the paperwork. Mrs. Shelly stayed in her office, and it was a relief not to hear her heels clicking. On the way back, Connie passed a closet marked JANITORIAL. She paused.

"Can't hurt to take a look," she mumbled to herself, turning the doorknob. It was locked.

"Well, that's that."

She took a few steps before stopping. This was neither the time nor place.

But she was here.

She'd take one quick look and then forget the whole thing. She kicked the door open. She didn't have time to pick the lock, and she could always pay for it later.

It was impossible to miss the giant hole in the floor and the ladder descending into it. Or the unearthly glow coming from within.

"Damn it."

Deeper into the hole, she recognized the strange hiero-glyphics of the lost continent of Mu along the carved walls.

She emerged from the tunnel into an antechamber, where three men in robes stood before an altar, chanting in Sumerian. An ancient idol to Nergal, Mesopotamian god of the under-world, sat on the altar pulsing with arcane energies.

"You're really better off leaving stuff like that alone," interrupted Connie.

The cultists, their faces twisted in rage, rose, drawing

daggers. Cultists never used guns, which always made things easier.

"You defile this sacred place, unbeliever," said one of the cultists. "And you shall pay with your life!"

The other two charged her. She took them both out.

The third grabbed the idol, holding it over his head. His body blazed with supernatural power as he cackled madly. "And now, I shall smite you!"

"Okay, so I hate to break this to you, but that is an idol to Nergal, god of the underworld."

"Yes, I know." His eyes burned red.

"And it just so happens that Nergal owes me a favor. Long story."

The idol flashed brighter, and the cultist disintegrated. Connie caught the idol as its supernatural energies faded.

"Okay, buddy," she said to the idol. "We're even now."

She tucked it under her arm. She was climbing halfway into the closet when the shadow of an old bald man in a janitor's jumpsuit fell over her. Mr. Pliskin sneered, holding a dagger over her head.

"You shall die for your sacrilege!"

Risky smacked Pliskin on the back of the head with the fire extinguisher. He stumbled, disoriented, giving Connie enough time to climb out of the hole and knock him out with a spin kick.

"Neat," said Risky.

"When you didn't come back, we came looking for you," Byron said.

"It was my idea," said Risky. "Can't be too careful with cultists running around."

Connie smiled. "No, you can't be too careful."

"So can you teach me kung fu?"

"Sure."

"Cool." Risky hoisted the fire extinguisher over her shoulder and walked away. "Cool."

Connie took Byron's hand. She wasn't nervous anymore.

"Yes," she said. "Cool."

About the Author

A. Lee Martinez is a writer, which is probably obvious. His novels are known for combining pulp and comic book influences along with philosophy, metaphysics, and humor. He describes his style as Saturday Morning Humanism. His novel *Monster* was adapted into the Chinese language film *Monster Run*. He isn't a very interesting person, but he likes very much writing and getting paid for it, so he's got that going for him. He lives outside of Dallas, Texas, with his wife and the minimum number of pets required as a writer.